PRAISE FOR

TALES OF THE FROG PRINCESS

"High-spirited romantic comedy. . . . Fans of Gail Carson Levine's 'Princess Tales' should leap for it."
—*Kirkus Reviews* on *The Frog Princess*

"Quests, tests, hearts won and broken, encounters with dragons, and plenty of magic . . .
As tasty as its prequel."
—*School Library Journal* on *Dragon's Breath*

"Baker's . . . vividly imagined fantasy world . . . [is] irresistible and loaded with humor."
—*VOYA* on *Once Upon a Curse*

"Kids will get a kick out of the hip *Shrek* vibe . . . in this updated fairy tale."
—*School Library Journal* on *No Place for Magic*

"An entertaining prequel. . . . An engaging main character . . . , sibling rivalries, and a romantic love interest combine in this appealing choice."
—*Booklist* on *The Salamander Spell*

BOOKS BY E. D. BAKER

Tales of the Frog Princess:
The Frog Princess
Dragon's Breath
Once Upon a Curse
No Place for Magic
The Salamander Spell
The Dragon Princess
Dragon Kiss
A Prince among Frogs
The Frog Princess Returns

Fairy Wings
Fairy Lies

Tales of the Wide-Awake Princess:
The Wide-Awake Princess
Unlocking the Spell
The Bravest Princess
Princess in Disguise
Princess Between Worlds
The Princess and the Pearl
Princess Before Dawn

A Question of Magic

The Fairy-Tale Matchmaker:
The Fairy-Tale Matchmaker
The Perfect Match
The Truest Heart
The Magical Match

More Than a Princess:
More Than a Princess
Power of a Princess

The Frog Princess

BOOK ONE IN THE
TALES OF THE FROG PRINCESS

E. D. BAKER

BLOOMSBURY
NEW YORK   LONDON   OXFORD   NEW DELHI   SYDNEY

First published in the United States of America in November 2002
by Bloomsbury Children's Books
Paperback edition published in October 2004
New edition published in August 2014
www.bloomsbury.com

Bloomsbury is a registered trademark of Bloomsbury Publishing Plc

For information about permission to reproduce selections from this book, write to
Permissions, Bloomsbury Children's Books, 1385 Broadway, New York, New York 10018
Bloomsbury books may be purchased for business or promotional use. For information
on bulk purchases please contact Macmillan Corporate and Premium Sales Department at
specialmarkets@macmillan.com

The Library of Congress has cataloged the hardcover edition as follows:
Baker, E. D.
The frog princess / E. D. Baker.
p. cm.
Summary: After reluctantly kissing a frog, an awkward fourteen-year-old princess suddenly
finds herself a frog, too, and sets off with the prince to seek the means—and the self-
confidence—to become human again.
ISBN-13: 978-1-58234-799-8 • ISBN-10: 1-58234-799-9 (hardcover)
[1. Fairy tales. 2. Frogs—Fiction. 3. Princesses—Fiction. 4. Princes—Fiction.
5. Witches—Fiction. 6. Humorous stories.] 1. Title.
PZ8.B173Fr2002   [Fic]—dc21   2002074506

ISBN 978-1-61963-617-0 (new edition) • ISBN 978-1-59990-398-9 (e-book)

Typeset by Dorchester Typesetting Group Ltd.
Printed and bound in the U.S.A. by Sheridan, Chelsea, Michigan
8   10   9

All papers used by Bloomsbury Publishing, Inc., are natural, recyclable products
made from wood grown in well-managed forests. The manufacturing processes
conform to the environmental regulations of the country of origin.

This book is dedicated to Ellie, Kimmy, and Nate
for their encouragement and support.
I would also like to thank Victoria Wells Arms,
Nancy Denton, and Rebecca Gardner
for their comments and suggestions.

One

ven as a little girl, I had thought that the swamp was a magical place where new lives began and old ones ended, where enemies and heroes weren't always what one expected, and where anything could happen, even to a clumsy princess. Although I'd believed this for most of my life, I had no proof until Prince Jorge came to visit and I met the frog of my dreams.

I had gone to the swamp to avoid the prince, a favorite of my mother's but never of mine. My escape hadn't been planned, yet the moment I heard that Jorge was coming, I knew I couldn't stay. Normally, few people in the castle ever seemed to notice me, so it was easy to sneak away undetected and flee to the swamp. It was only after I was secure in my escape that I began to worry about how my mother would react. I could almost see the disdain in her eyes as she gave me her usual speech about the proper behavior of a princess. Although I saw her as infrequently as we both could manage, I'd long since grown accustomed to that look.

Thinking more about my mother than I was about my surroundings, I almost stepped on a snake that had slithered onto the path from the tall grass. I shrieked and jumped back, catching my heel on the root of an old willow tree. With my arms flung wide, I tried to keep my balance, but my long, heavy skirts and usual clumsiness overwhelmed me and I landed hard on the rain-soaked earth. Grasshoppers exploded up from the ground as I floundered about, struggling to get to my feet, my gown soaking in the pungent odor of the swamp. Unfortunately, being born a princess doesn't automatically make a girl graceful or confident, a fact I've lamented for most of my fourteen years.

When I'd finally gathered my skirts and pushed myself off the ground, the snake had disappeared into the tall swamp grass. I edged away, searching for something that I could use to defend myself should the snake reappear.

"Thanks a lot!" said a throaty voice.

I looked around, but there was no one in sight. "Who said that?" I asked. Aside from my aunt Grassina, I was the only one from the castle who ever visited the swamp.

"It's me, over here. You aren't very observant, are you?"

I turned toward the voice and looked high and low, but all I could see was the pond, its murky water partially rimmed with a halo of algae, and a stand of cattails at the far end. Aside from the dragonflies, mosquitoes, and water striders, the only other living creature was a frog glaring at me from the edge of the pond. I jumped when he spoke again, although it wasn't so much his words that surprised me as seeing his lips move. I'm used to magic, for my aunt Grassina is a witch, but no animal had ever spoken to me before.

"I was going to eat those grasshoppers for lunch, but because of you I'll never catch them now!" The frog scowled, shaking his webbed finger in my direction. "A big, galumphing girl like you should be more careful where she puts her feet!"

"I'm sorry," I said, offended. "I didn't mean to. It was an accident."

"Hah!" said the frog. "Apologies won't bring back my lunch! But then, it wouldn't matter to you, would it? I bet you've never gone hungry a day in your life!"

The frog annoyed me. It was enough that I had to watch my tongue around my mother. I wasn't about to do it around a frog as well. "For your information," I said, frowning at the little creature, "I haven't eaten a thing all day. My mother invited Prince Jorge to visit and I left home before he arrived. I couldn't bear the thought of spending an entire day with him."

"What is wrong with you?" demanded the frog, curling his lip. "Missing a meal because you don't like someone! You would never catch me doing that! I know Jorge and even he isn't ..." The frog blinked and his eyes opened wide. He leaned closer, scrutinizing me from head to toe as if seeing me for the first time. "Wait a minute ... If your mother invited a prince to visit, does that mean that you're a princess?"

"Maybe," I said.

The frog grinned from eardrum to eardrum. Straightening his smooth green shoulders, he bowed from where his waist would have been if he'd had one. "I do apologize, Your Highness! If I had realized that you were such an exalted personage, I would never have made such churlish comments."

I groaned and rolled my eyes. "Give me a break. I hate it when people talk that way. I liked you better before you knew I was a princess."

"Ah-hah!" said the frog. He hopped toward me, his eyes never leaving my face. "I'm delighted to hear that you like me! In that case, would you be so kind as to do me the eensy-weensiest little favor?"

"And what might that be?" I asked, regretting my question even before the words were out of my mouth.

"Would you do me the honor of giving me a kiss?"

I couldn't help but laugh. I guffawed, I chortled, I wheezed. I laughed like I always do. Startled blackbirds took to the air as if hurled from a little boy's slingshot. A turtle basking in the sun scuttled off his rock and plopped into the water. The frog stared at me through narrowed eyes. "Are you sure you're a princess? You don't laugh like one."

"I know," I said, wiping away tears. "My mother tells me that all the time. According to her, a princess's laughter should sound like the tinkling of a bell, not the bray of a donkey. I've told her that I can't help it. My laugh is not something I can control, not if it's sincere. I don't think about it. It just happens."

"Whatever you say," said the frog. "So how about that kiss?" Puckering his lips, he rose up on his toes and raised his face in my direction.

I shook my head. "Sorry, I'm not interested in kissing a frog."

"I've been told that kissing a frog is good for the complexion," he said, sidling toward me.

"I doubt it. Anyway, my complexion is fine."

"What about the old saying, kissing a frog would bring you luck?"

"I've never heard that saying. It can't be too old. I think you just made it up. All kissing a frog would bring me is slimy lips." I shuddered and backed away. "The answer is no, so quit asking!"

The frog sighed and scratched the side of his head with his toe. "Maybe you would feel otherwise if you knew that I was a prince turned into a frog by an evil witch. I had the misfortune to criticize her fashion sense.

She didn't take kindly to my comments."

"What does that have to do with a kiss?"

"If I can get a princess to kiss me, I'll turn back into a prince!"

"That's not very flattering to me, now, is it? All you need is a kiss from any old princess. A girl likes to think that her very first kiss will be something special. Well, I'm not going to kiss you! I have no idea where you've been. I could catch some awful disease. Besides, considering what you must eat, I bet you have awful breath."

"Well!" said the frog. He drew himself up to his full froggy height. "Now you're being rude. I simply asked you for the courtesy of a small favor and instead you insult me."

"That was a big favor and you know it. I kiss only people I like, and I just met you!"

"But this is important. It's a matter of life or frog-hood!"

"I'm sorry. I'm not in the habit of kissing strangers, regardless of their species. Can't you get someone else to kiss you? There must be another princess you could ask. Someone petite who doesn't trip over her own feet." Although I wasn't about to admit it to the frog, his comment about my size still rankled. I had heard the same kind of remark from my mother many times, but it never stopped bothering me.

"Sure! I'll ask one of the hundreds of other

princesses who are hanging around the swamp, begging to be kissed!"

I'd had enough. Gathering my skirts in one hand, I turned to go. "If that's the way you're going to be, I'm leaving. I left the castle today so I wouldn't have to visit with an obnoxious prince. Now here I am, talking to an obnoxious frog who says he's a prince."

"No! Wait! Come back!" called the frog. "You can't go now! This is an emergency! Where's your compassion? Where's your sympathy? Where's my kiss?"

I stopped at the edge of the path and tried to speak in a calm voice. It wasn't easy, and I'm afraid my words came out sounding short and sharp. "I don't care if it's the end of the world as we know it," I said between gritted teeth. "I have better things to do with my time than listen to unreasonable requests from a frog. Good day, Frog."

The last thing I saw before I turned to leave was the hopeless look in the frog's eyes. It was the look of someone in terrible trouble. It was a look that would haunt me for the rest of the day.

Two

 spent the rest of the afternoon visiting my favorite places in the swamp. Following hidden pathways, I skirted the treacherous, boggy ground until I reached solid footing. After searching the thicket where I'd stumbled across twin fawns earlier that spring, I lounged by the deep pool that mirrored the drifting, puffball clouds. As the day grew warmer, I took off my shoes and stockings and waded through a shallow stream to a tiny island whose smooth, water-tumbled pebbles felt good under my bare feet.

It was late by the time I returned to the castle. Rather than going straight to my bedchamber, I climbed the long, narrow tower steps to my aunt Grassina's apartments. The Green Witch, as she is called, is my mother's sister and has lived in the castle since before I was born. She has taught me more than anyone else ever has, and not just about how to be a princess. And unlike the rest of my family, she doesn't criticize me at every opportunity.

Reaching the top of the stairs, I knocked softly on the door and waited for her to answer. Somehow, she always knew who was knocking. She'd told me how useful a skill that was, because she wouldn't have to answer the door if it were someone she didn't want to see. After only a few seconds the door flew open, but instead of my aunt's familiar features I saw a yellow duckling drop a gnawed stick and rush out of the room to snap at my ankles.

"Come back here, Bowser!" my aunt called from inside the room. "I'm not finished with you yet!"

The duckling darted back and forth, quacking loudly as it herded me over the threshold.

"Shut the door, Emeralda!" shouted my aunt from her seat by her workbench. "That stupid dog won't hold still long enough for me to finish the spell!"

"This is Bowser?" I asked, trying to fend off the ball of fluff that was viciously attacking the toe of my shoe. "Father won't be happy that you turned his favorite hound into a duck."

"Duck, dog, what's the difference? Bowser will be his miserable self again faster than you can say the Greek alphabet backward. Now, where was I? Oh, yes. Here, sprinkle some of this on him while I find the spell again."

"What, me? I can't!" I backed away from her outstretched hand. "I'll make a mess of it! Remember that

9

time with the crab apple dumplings?" After I used that spell to make them, they grew claws and ran away. It took us weeks to find the crabby little things, and by then they were stale and their claws had pinched us black and blue.

"Phooey," said Aunt Grassina. "Everybody makes mistakes."

"But not the kind I make! I used that cleaning spell you told me about nearly four months ago and it's still as strong as ever! Every time I drop anything on the floor in my chamber, a little breeze whisks it away and dumps it on the dung heap behind the stables. You wouldn't believe how many stockings and hairpins I've lost that way! I can't do magic anymore. I just make things worse when I do."

"How do you ever think you'll learn to be a witch if you don't try?"

"I don't want to be a witch!" I said for the hundredth time. "I know you think I should, but I'd be terrible at it. If I could mess up such simple cooking and cleaning spells, imagine what I could do with something really important. We could all end up with three left feet or stuck head-down in some desert!"

"Oh, Emma! Of course you want to be a witch! You just don't know it yet. Give yourself some time and a little more practice. I'm sure you'll be very good at it once you decide to apply yourself. Now, where is that parchment? I know I put it around here somewhere."

I left my aunt shuffling through a stack of old, musty parchments and headed toward my favorite chair in front of the fireplace. The truth was, I used to dream about being a witch like Grassina, but to try so hard for so long and never have anything go quite right ... I slumped into the chair and closed my eyes, letting my bad day melt away in the peace of Grassina's room.

The difference between my aunt's room and the rest of the castle was wonderful. Whereas the castle itself was cold and damp and generally gloomy, Grassina's room was warm and inviting. A small fire always burned behind the decorated iron grate, heating the entire room, yet never needing new logs. Gleaming balls of witches' light bumped against the ceiling, bathing the white-washed walls and brightly colored tapestries with a rosy glow. The cold stone floors were covered with thick, woven rugs of various shades of green, giving it the appearance of a forest floor dappled with sunlight. Sometimes the room smelled of freshly crushed mint leaves, or pine boughs like the ones used to decorate the Great Hall during the winter celebrations, or sun-warmed clover on a summer's day.

Two chairs cushioned for comfort and separated by a small table waited in front of the hearth. A fragrant bouquet of crystalline flowers bloomed in an etched bowl atop the table. A gift from the fairies, the bouquet was the home to glass butterflies whose delicate wings clicked softly as they flitted from one blossom to another. I'd spent many hours curled up in one of the chairs while my aunt occupied the other, regaling me with stories of far-off lands and times long ago.

There were many wonders to be found in my aunt's room. One of her tapestries depicted a miniature town in perfect detail with a lion and a unicorn fighting each other in the streets. Once, when I touched the lion with my fingertip, it bit me, taking a small sliver of skin from my finger. I howled as tears streamed down my face. My mother cuffed me for lying, but Grassina winked and wrapped my wound in spider's silk.

A sea witch named Coral had given Grassina a large bowl filled with salt water and the tiny replica of a castle, spires and all. The castle was perfect in every detail, and occasionally I'd see schools of miniature fish swimming by.

Sometimes, when I'd visit after the sun had set, I saw lights glowing in the tiny windows of the castle. Even so, I never would have thought it more than an interesting curiosity if I hadn't come to visit my aunt one winter's afternoon when I was nine or so. Having taken longer than usual to answer my knock, she came to the door with dripping hair and a cloth she was using to dry it. The entire room smelled strongly of fish, but when I asked what she'd been doing, she smiled and left the room to change her clothes. As I moved to warm my hands by the fireplace, I stepped in a damp patch on the floor and thought that the salt water in the bowl had overflowed. Glancing at the bowl, I saw a flash of silver and blue. I hurried closer to peer into the water, just as the diminutive figure of a mermaid reached one of the tiny doors. Jerking the door open, she turned to look over her shoulder and saw me. Her eyes grew wide in alarm and she darted through the opening, slamming the door behind her. I began to think that the bowl might contain more than it appeared.

The duckling quacked, a surprising sound in the quiet room. I opened my eyes and sat up, turning toward my aunt Grassina. She was perched on a tall stool facing a massive wooden table, ignoring the duckling as it gnawed on the table leg. An old quill pen stuck out of Grassina's thick chestnut hair, the same color as mine.

I've been told that Grassina and I look much alike, but whereas her nose is thin and refined, mine is prominent like my father's. Her eyes are green, a shade or two lighter than my own. Grassina's smile is beautiful on the rare occasion when she treats us to one. However, her smile never seems to reach her eyes. My old nanny, long since retired, told me that Grassina was quite cheerful in her youth but that time and my grandmother had taken their toll.

Grassina always wore green and her gown on this day was the color of summer moss. Shapeless and loose, it had no certain style, hanging limply from her tall frame. My aunt always dressed as she pleased, never worrying about what others might think. I was not so fortunate; my mother never let me forget that a princess is always on display.

I watched as Grassina, caught up in her work, used both hands to hold a partially unrolled parchment. Other parchments littered the table and spilled onto the floor. The last rays of the setting sun slanted through the window to pool on the surface of the table and turn her farseeing ball, just like the one she'd given me, into a dazzling sphere of light. A small apple-green snake lay coiled among the parchments, soaking up the sun's warmth.

"What are those for?" I asked. I hopped out of my chair and crossed the room to stand beside my aunt. The snake raised its head and flicked its tongue in my direction. Shuddering, I stepped back a pace or two. Although the creature had lived with my aunt for many years, I had never grown used to its presence. There were few things I feared in the world more than snakes, regardless of the temperament or type.

"I was cataloging my parchments when I came across the spell for ducklings. I thought I'd try it out and Bowser just happened to be handy. Now, where is that spell? I know it was in one of these....

"So," she said, turning around in her seat and raising

an eyebrow. "I have a feeling you have a question for me. You do have a question, don't you?"

"Have you ever turned anyone into something like, say, a frog?"

"Certainly. Human-to-frog is a simple spell and easy to remember. I've used it many times myself. Why do you ask?"

"I've met a frog who claims to be a prince, and I was wondering if he might be telling the truth."

"Now, that would be hard to say. He could be a prince, but then again he could simply be a talking frog. Some witches have strange senses of humor. I should know."

"Say he is a prince. What would he have to do to go back to being human?"

"That depends on the witch who cast the spell. But whatever it takes, she would have had to tell him. The spell won't work if there is no remedy or if she doesn't tell him what it is. However, the usual method involves asking a maiden, preferably a princess, for a kiss. I'm surprised you didn't know that. When I was young, kissing a frog was the only way some girls got dates. I myself spent too much time searching ponds and marshes for frogs to kiss. Of course, I was looking for one in particular at the time."

"You mean Haywood, your old beau?"

"You remember that story, do you? Yes, it's true.

After I brought him home to meet your grandmother, she took a dislike to him and he disappeared for good. I was convinced that she'd turned him into a frog. Your grandmother was never a very imaginative person. But try as I did, I never found my darling Haywood. I'd given up eating and sleeping and spent all of my time searching the swamp, kissing every frog I could catch. My mother finally made me stop by threatening to lock me in an abandoned tower in the middle of nowhere unless I returned to my studies. He wasn't just my beau, you know. We were engaged to be married. He was the only man I've ever loved."

"So to turn a frog back into a prince …," I said, trying to get the conversation back on track.

"Oh, yes, well, it doesn't have to be a kiss. It could be anything, within limits. If a spell were too easy to break, it wouldn't be strong enough to last. If breaking it were impossible, it would go against the natural laws of magic and also wouldn't last. There is a certain degree of fairness involved, you know. Speaking of fairness, do you think that you were being fair when you took off this morning, leaving me to deal with your mother? Chartreuse was madder than a wet peacock when no one could find you. I told her I had sent you on an errand, so now she's angry with me again."

"Sorry about that," I said, avoiding her eyes. "And thank you for covering for me. Mother had invited

Prince Jorge to visit. Jorge spends all of his time bragging and acting as if I don't exist. I didn't see why I needed to be there. Jorge never talks to me anyway. As far as he's concerned, I might as well be a piece of furniture."

Bowser was scratching at my aunt's skirts with his webbed foot while making an odd whining sound. When she ignored him, he wandered off and attacked the table leg, his little bill clacking against the wood.

"Well, I don't mind this time," Grassina told me, brushing a stray lock of hair from her eyes, "but you'll have to face her one of these days. I won't always be around to cover for you like I was today. It's getting late and I doubt you've had a thing to eat. You'd better go get yourself something from the kitchen. I don't have time to cook for you and I'll never get anything done with you here distracting me. Now, where did I put that parchment?"

Three

The next morning I was out of bed and dressed long before the rest of the household was stirring. Wearing my dark blue gown with my pale blue kirtle, and carrying my third-best shoes in my hand, I tiptoed down the stairs, shivering at the icy chill of the stone. According to her maid, my mother had gone to bed with a headache the previous night. I had yet to see her. Coward that I was, I was determined to be out of the castle and away from the grounds before she could corner me about the previous day's disappearance.

The sun was peeking over the distant hills when I reached the edge of the swamp. A lone mosquito circled my head, whining in its high-pitched, irritating way. Tripping on my own feet, I stumbled into the underbrush and stirred up a cloud of its relatives. The blackflies swarmed as I neared the pond, but because I'd used a bitter-smelling salve that Grassina had made to repel them, none of the insects landed on me. Even so, the persistent whining began to get on my nerves. I flapped my hand to swat them away, and to my surprise, I connected with a large fly, knocking it over the water.

Thwip! A long, froggy tongue flicked out and snagged the fly. "Thanks!" said a familiar voice. "I needed that!"

"I wasn't trying to feed you," I said. "I just hate these obnoxious bugs."

"Really?" said the frog. "I think they're delightful, although some are a little too salty. So tell me, did you sleep well last night or did your conscience bother you for abandoning me in my hour of need?"

"No, I didn't sleep well...."

"Ah-hah!"

"But it had nothing to do with my conscience. It was curiosity more than anything. I was wondering—exactly who is it you claim to be?"

"I am His Royal Highness, Prince Eadric of Upper Montevista." Bowing, the frog fluttered his hand in a noble gesture. "So what do you say?" he asked, looking up. "How about that kiss?"

"Just because you say you're Prince Eadric doesn't mean you really are. Traveling minstrels are awful gossips, and I would have heard if a prince had been turned into a frog."

"Only if people knew what had happened. I doubt my family has any knowledge of the calamity that befell me. Then again," he said under his breath, "they might know what happened and are trying to cover it up. That happens a lot in my family."

"Mine, too," I said. "You should see how fast my mother can make an embarrassing situation disappear. You'd almost think that she was the witch instead of Aunt Grassina."

"You have an aunt who's a witch?" the frog asked, becoming agitated. "Is she ... Is she really ugly with hair like a thistle? Is she mean and nasty and cruel to innocent fashion critics?"

"No, nothing like that. My aunt Grassina is wonderful! She's the best relative anybody could have. Grassina is the only one in my family who doesn't ridicule me for being clumsy. She doesn't expect me to be the perfect little lady every minute of the day, and she's taught me a lot of useful things that no one else would ever have thought of teaching me. And her presents! My parents always give me boring presents like clothes on my birthdays, but aunt Grassina gives me much more interesting things, like my farseeing ball and a bottomless bottle of perfume and this beautiful charm bracelet." I shook my wrist for emphasis, making my bracelet jingle merrily. "Grassina told me what the symbols mean, but I was only a little girl then, so I don't really remember. I love it, though. It glows in the dark and I wear it all the time, even at night."

Mosquitoes tickled my scalp, the one place I hadn't

put any salve. When I tried to brush them away with my hand, one of my combs fell out and landed in the mud. I reached for it and it came out with a squelch, splattering my sleeve with muddy droplets. "Listen, I'd better go now. If you're Eadric, you're going to have to prove it."

"How?"

"I don't know. Think of something. I'll come back when I can."

I hurried off with the insects pursuing me all the way home. It didn't seem to matter where I was—it just wasn't going to be an easy morning. I knew I couldn't put off facing my mother any longer, and my stomach was already tying itself in knots. I tried to distract myself by thinking of the frog's request. If he really was Prince Eadric, he was in big trouble and needed my help. I couldn't stand to see any animal suffer, whether he was an enchanted prince or not. And if it was all a trick, well, I needed to know that, too. I already made a fool of myself too often without someone else doing it for me.

My mother must have alerted all the servants to watch for me: as soon as I set foot on the castle grounds the head gardener intercepted me and hustled me off to my mother's chamber. For someone who had been anxious to see me, my mother didn't seem very pleased.

"So there you are!" she said, looking me over from head to toe just as she always did. "Stand up straight, Emeralda! Don't slouch! Look at you! Your hair is a mess, your dress is soiled, and you have mud on your shoes." My mother lifted her chin and sniffed daintily, her delicate nostrils flaring only the tiniest bit, the barely discernable wrinkles around her eyes deepening only slightly.

"Good morning, Mother. I'm sorry I displease you."

"You've been off to that dreadful swamp again, I see." Mother curled her lip in disgust.

"Yes, Mother," I said, focusing on one of Mother's carefully crafted curls. She spent hours on her appearance each morning, and I had never seen her without her honey-gold hair looking perfect.

"It's a pity you weren't around yesterday. I had a lovely visit with Prince Jorge. He really is quite charming."

"Yes, Mother," I said, barely able to force the words past my lips. Although I'd seen him be charming to other people, he'd never acted that way toward me. The first time I met him I tripped entering the room. Instead of helping me up, he laughed, making me feel even more like an idiot. Our relationship had only gone downhill from there.

"I've done something wonderful for you, child, and you will, of course, thank me for it."

"Thank you, Mother," I said, wondering what it could be. The last time I'd had to thank her without knowing what I was thanking her for, I'd been ill and she'd invited a bloodletter to put leeches on me. I hoped there were no leeches involved this time, although with my mother, anything was possible.

Mother smiled smugly as she adjusted the lace on her sleeve. "I've begun engagement negotiations. We've tentatively scheduled the wedding for the end of the summer."

My heart sank. Marry Prince Jorge? I couldn't believe that anyone might think that we were suitable for each other. I was clumsy in social situations and terrified of talking in public, never knowing quite what to say. Jorge was poised and handsome and so full of himself that even his horse had to kneel when his master entered the stable. I began to think that the arrival of the bloodletter and his leeches might have been better news.

"But I can't marry Jorge! We don't love each other!"

My mother gave me a look so cold that I stepped back a pace. "What does that have to do with anything?" she asked. "Husbands and wives who love each other are the exception, not the rule. Stop whining and be happy that he wants your hand at all. Not many princes would be willing to marry someone as awkward as you. Despite all my efforts, you have few social graces. If only you'd been born a boy as your father and I had wanted! Maybe then I could have made something of you. As it is, this match is the best that you can hope for, so I expect you to be gracious about it. Now see what you've done! I can feel my headache returning."

Marrying Jorge would be a terrible mistake. I was beginning to feel so desperate that I was unable to let the subject drop. "Mother," I said, "Jorge is a fool! I can't marry him!'"

"Many women have married fools and been perfectly happy. Negotiations have begun and despite what you may think, they do not require your approval. You should be glad that I care enough to arrange a marriage for you at all. Now, hurry and fetch my maid. My head is pounding."

I was devastated. To think that my mother wanted me to leave my beautiful swamp and marry that horrid Prince Jorge! After sending my mother's maid to her, I went in search of my aunt Grassina, but the door to her tower room was locked. A dripping sign written in red berry juice had been nailed to the thick wood.

> Beware, all ye who would trespass here.
> Those who set foot beyond this portal
> uninvited shall have their hearts ripped
> out by dragons and their brains eaten by
> maggots. Deliverymen, please leave all
> packages by the door. Emeralda, I've been
> called away for a few days. I'll let you
> know when I get back. We'll make your
> favorite fruit tarts.
>
> Grassina, the Green Witch

I had to talk to someone about my mother's dreadful plans. I went in search of a friend who wasn't too busy to talk to me, but I didn't have much luck. Fortunata, the daughter of mother's favorite lady-in-waiting, was sick in bed with a cold and couldn't be disturbed, which was just as well, for she was a terrible snob herself and probably would have considered Prince Jorge a great catch. Violet, the scullery maid, was scrubbing the kitchen floor for the second time that day and was not in a good mood. Bernard, the undergardener, was being scolded for failing to rid the garden of slugs. Chloe, the second-best seamstress, was helping the head seamstress sew yet another gown for my mother. I tried to think of someone else I could talk to, someone who wouldn't be too busy or impatient for a real conversation. Somehow, I kept thinking about the obnoxious little frog in the swamp. He was rude and sarcastic, but at least he wanted to talk to me.

Hurrying back to the swamp, I was surprised at how eager I was to see the frog again. When I saw him sitting on his lily pad, I smiled for the first time that day.

"Couldn't stay away, huh?" he said as soon as he saw me. "Sorry, I haven't thought of any proof yet, although I could tell you about some of my exploits. I'm sure the minstrels are singing about them already. For instance, there was the time that I—"

"Never mind that now. I just have to talk to someone! You'll never guess what awful thing my mother has done!"

"She nailed all of your shoes to the floor."

"Of course not! Why would she do that?"

"She had a servant wash all of your whites with red stockings!"

"Whatever are you talking about? You aren't even close!"

"She ordered you to kiss the first frog you met!" the frog said, batting his eyelids at me.

"Not in a million years! I told you you'd never guess it. She's arranging for me to marry Prince Jorge!"

"You're kidding! I can't imagine anyone marrying Jorge. He's so in love with himself that there's no room for anyone else in the relationship. Have you ever seen the way he looks at his own reflection in a looking glass? It's enough to make a dog sick! And confidentially," whispered the frog after looking around to make sure that no one else was listening, "I've heard that Jorge has a fondness for ladies' shoes. He has a whole trunk of them that he keeps locked in his bedchamber!"

"I don't know about that, but I do know that I can't marry him. He's a rude idiot who barely acknowledges my existence. I could never be happy married to someone like that! Besides, he makes me so nervous I get all tongue-tied and can't think of what to say."

"You don't seem to have any problem talking to me," said the frog.

"You're different. It's easy to talk to you. You're just a frog."

"I'm a prince, too!"

"Maybe, but you don't look like one. You don't act like one, either, so it's easy to forget. But Jorge is something else. He never lets you forget that he's a prince."

"Maybe if you talk to your mother ..."

"It wouldn't make a bit of difference if I did. Appearance is everything to my mother. I know she won't change her mind. And my father will do whatever she says just so he doesn't have to argue with her. How could my mother do this to me? Why, I'd rather marry you than Prince Jorge, whether you're a prince or not. You wouldn't ignore me or laugh at me, would you?"

The frog blinked in surprise. "No, of course not."

"See? And at least if I married you, I wouldn't have to leave the swamp!"

"Gee," said the frog, looking flustered. "I don't know. All I asked for was a kiss."

"You want a kiss? Fine! I'll give you a kiss. I'd rather kiss you than Prince Jorge any day!"

I knelt on the ground at the edge of the pond. With a mighty leap, the frog landed on the ground beside me and puckered his lips.

"Wait just a minute," I said, drawing back.

The frog looked distressed. "You haven't changed your mind, have you?"

"No, no, it's just that ... well, here." Fumbling in the small pouch attached to the waist of my gown, I found an embroidered handkerchief. I reached out and gently patted the frog's mouth clean. "You had dried fly feet stuck to your lips," I said, shuddering. "All right, let's try again."

This time the kiss went without a hitch. I leaned down, puckered my lips, and closed my eyes. Violet, who had had far more experience than I, had told me you should always do that when kissing a boy. I assumed it was the same when kissing a boy frog. The frog's lips felt cool and smooth against mine. The sensation wasn't too unpleasant. It was what happened next that took me by surprise.

The tingling began in my fingers and toes, then spread up my arms and legs. A shiver ran up my spine, chased by a golden, fuzzy feeling. Suddenly, my head felt light and full of bubbles. A tremendous wind rushed past me, knocking me to the ground. I covered my face with my arms, but my arms no longer felt real. When I tried to stand, my whole body shook, and a gray cloud filled my head.

Four

I opened my eyes and blinked. My head felt woozy; nothing would come into focus. Gradually my vision sharpened, but everything looked different somehow. The colors seemed brighter and there were more of them. An enormous butterfly flew past, its wings seesawing up and down through the air. It wore beautiful reds and shades of purple that I'd never seen before.

"Oh!" I said aloud, and flinched at the timbre of my own voice. It sounded strange in my ears and talking made my throat feel funny.

My nostrils flared at the sour smell of decaying vegetation and swamp muck. The leaves in the trees rattled loudly in the wind while the hum of a million insects nearly deafened me. *Thump!* Something heavy hit the damp soil by the edge of the pond. *Thump!* It came again, louder and closer. Heavy breathing filled the air.

I tried to stand, but my legs wouldn't cooperate. Still dazed, I looked down. The ground was much closer than it had been only a few moments ago; the clumps of dirt were larger as well. A pair of webbed feet and long, muscular legs stretched out in front of me. Puzzled, I squeezed my eyes shut, then opened them to look again. The legs were attached to a short, plump body covered with mottled, green skin. My brain refused to acknowledge what my eyes told me. I lifted my hand and wiggled my fingers. Four green, crooked fingers twitched. Suddenly, I understood: I wasn't looking at some other creature. I was looking at myself!

"What's this? What's happened? How did this—" I babbled. My heart raced as panic set in. "I'm dreaming, that's it! I'm home in bed and I'm dreaming!"

Thump! Whatever I'd heard before was coming closer. I squeezed my eyes shut and pressed my body to the ground. "I'm imagining this. If I ignore it, it'll go away," I said aloud. My mother had often derided me for having a vivid imagination, but this was too much even for me!

Thump! Thump! Thump! Something large and wet pressed against my back, snuffling hot, smelly air from my head to my feet. *It's so real,* I thought, and opened first one eye, then the other. An enormous white dog with short, dirty fur loomed over me, studying me intently with its huge, red-rimmed eyes. My father's dogs were all brown or black or gray. This dog was a stranger to me and therefore all the more frightening. I shuddered as it pushed me with its nose, tumbling me over onto my side. It snuffled me once more, then opened its cavernous mouth wide. My stomach churned from the smell of the dog's breath. A big drop of hot, stinky slobber dripped onto my head.

This is not a dream, I thought. With a convulsive twitch, I rolled to my feet and leaped as far and as fast as I could. My movements were clumsy and uncoordinated, but I leaped again and again, each time putting more and more distance between the dog and myself. One final leap, a half twist, and a flop, and I landed in the water with a splash.

"Frog!" said the dog as it belly-flopped into the water after me. "Come back! I need to talk to you!"

Too frightened to answer the dog, I flailed my arms and tried to get away. Although I'd grown up near the water, I had never learned how to swim. As clumsy as I was, I was sure that if I ever stepped in water that went higher than my ankles I would drown. I floundered, thrashing my arms and legs and going nowhere. The dog lunged for me again, creating a wave that washed me toward the middle of the pond. Drawing up my legs, I kicked hard and shot through the water, away from the dog and its crushing jaws. *It worked!* I thought, surprised at myself. I did it again. The water rushed past as I hurtled forward, barely missing a tiny sunfish. I twisted around and rose to the surface to look for the dog.

31

Dashing back and forth in the shallow water at the edge of the pond, the beast was no longer a threat.

A wave of relief washed over me. *I did it!* I thought. *I got away from that giant dog all on my own! I can do anything!* Gleefully, I twirled around in the water. I splashed from one side of the pond to the other, and when I grew tired of kicking, I ducked my head and blew bubbles. Floating on my stomach, I watched the minnows dart past in frenzied formation. I enjoyed every minute of it, delighting in the sensation of the warm water coursing against my skin. As a princess, I had never been able to go outside unencumbered by heavy fabric and long skirts. The new feeling of freedom was exhilarating!

Eventually, I rolled onto my back and gazed up at the wispy clouds high in the clear blue sky. I wondered what had happened to Frog. I hadn't seen him since my transformation. It occurred to me that maybe it was a trick. Maybe we had switched places and he was now a human. But how could that have happened without my seeing it? Besides, although he might be obnoxious, I didn't think he was sneaky.

I climbed onto a partially submerged log, and thought about all that had happened that day. In the excitement of my escape from the dog and the discovery of my newfound abilities, I hadn't really thought about what I would do next. I was alone in the swamp with no one to turn to. What was I going to *do?*

Distraught, I hunched down and began to cry. I hated crying and almost never did. My mother had told me many times that a princess should never cry in public, but I knew that sometimes a person just couldn't help it. Large tears rolled down my cheeks and plopped onto the rough bark of the log. I was so miserable that I didn't notice Frog climb up beside me.

Five

"What's wrong?" Frog asked. He had to ask me twice before the question pierced my bubble of misery.

"Oh," I said, peering at him through tear-filled eyes. "It's you."

"I'm glad you're so thrilled to see me," Frog said. "But you still haven't answered my question. What's wrong? Why are you crying?"

"Isn't it obvious?" I asked. "I'm a frog and it's your fault! This wasn't supposed to happen. You said you would turn back into a prince. You never said I could turn into a frog!"

"What do I look like, a gypsy fortune-teller? No one ever told me this might happen. I'm sorry. I can't imagine why it did. But it's not so bad, you know. Being a frog, that is. I've been a frog for quite a while. It really does have its advantages."

"Oh?" I sniffled. "Like what?"

Frog shrugged. "You won't have to marry Jorge, for one. Life is less complicated as a frog. Why, I can do whatever I want to, like stay up all night or sleep all day. I don't have all the responsibilities or the worries that I used to have, either. You can't imagine how much of a relief it is not to be asked to slay a dragon or behead an ogre or shut down the troll extortion rings under the bridges, although I must admit that I was very good at all three. Now I only have to worry about finding enough food and being eaten."

"Those sound like pretty serious worries to me," I said.

"Not if you keep your wits about you and pay attention to what's going on. Which is something you need to learn to do."

"I guess I have been a little preoccupied."

"Do you think so? Come on! A dozen dragons could have landed here and toasted you for lunch and you wouldn't have noticed. You're lucky that I'm the one who climbed onto this log! But don't worry. I got you into this, so I'll teach you what you need to know."

"You don't have to teach me anything! Just undo whatever you did and turn me back into a princess!"

"I wish I could," said Frog. "Except I have no idea how to do it."

"Then you'll have to help me find out! I may not have been the happiest princess, but I don't want to spend the rest of my life as a frog! I can't believe this

happened! At first I thought it was all a dream, but ...
Say, where did you go, anyway? I didn't see you around
when that dog came."

Frog shrugged his smooth green shoulders. "When
you kissed me and I didn't become my handsome,
princely self again, I admit I was a little upset. It took a
while before I noticed that you weren't around anymore,
at least as a human. By the time I realized what must have
happened, that dog was there and you were hopping
around like a lunatic. You disappeared, but it was easy to
find you since everyone in the swamp was gossiping
about the crazy talking female frog who couldn't swim
any better than a newly hatched tadpole."

"I thought I swam quite well!" I said, remembering
my pride in my newly learned skill.

"Maybe for a rank beginner."

I couldn't help it. My lip began to quiver.

"Don't do that!" he said. "This is fresh water and
you're going to make it salty!"

Two big tears rolled down my cheeks. I sniffled
louder.

"Now what's wrong?" Frog asked impatiently.

"Everything!" I wailed. "I've been trying so hard and
I thought I was a good swimmer and now you tell me that
I'm not and I'm a frog and I don't want to be and I'm
scared and now on top of everything else I'm hungry!"

"Maybe if you kissed me again, you'd feel better,"

said Frog, leaning toward me.

"What?" I said, so surprised that I stopped crying. "Why would I want to do that?"

"It might cheer you up."

"I don't think so!"

"Well, then, maybe we'd be lucky and it would reverse the spell."

"And maybe we'd be unlucky and something worse would happen, although I can't imagine anything worse than being turned into a frog." I began to sniffle again.

"So!" Frog said quickly. "You said you're hungry. Now, that's something we can fix."

"What do you eat?" I asked, rubbing my eyelids with my fingers.

"Whatever comes along. Just watch me. You'll get the idea."

Frog hopped to the tip of the log and sat motionless. He sat still for so long that by the time he finally made his move, I'd become bored and fidgety and almost missed seeing what he did. A dragonfly about the length of a grown man's thumb zigzagged past the end of the log. Without warning, Frog leaped, opened his mouth, and flicked out his tongue. Before he hit the water, Frog had curled his tongue back into his mouth, dragging the dragonfly with it.

"You expect me to do that?" I asked incredulously when Frog rejoined me on the log.

"Only if you want to eat," Frog replied, licking his lips. "Look," he said, holding up the dragonfly's wings. "Aren't they beauties? If we were near my pad, I'd add them to my collection."

"You collect those things?"

"Are you kidding? I'm becoming quite an expert, if I do say so myself. My collection is probably the largest and most comprehensive in the world. Now look over there. See that big, juicy fly headed this way? Go ahead, I'll let you have it."

"I'm not eating a fly!" My stomach churned at the thought.

"You will when you get hungry enough. Watch me. I'll show you one more time."

"You can show me a million times, but that doesn't mean I'm going to do it. Isn't there anything else to eat besides bugs?"

"Hmm," said Frog. "I'll tell you what. I know a spot where there's lots to eat, but we're going to have to swim to get there."

"Fine with me," I said. "As long as I don't have to eat flies."

Frog grinned. "Stay near me and do what I do." He hopped to the edge of the log and plopped into the water. I followed close behind, worried that I might lose sight of him.

With Frog leading the way, we headed back

downstream. Swimming with the current was much easier, and I was surprised at how quickly we reached the pond. Suddenly, Frog motioned for me to stop, and even though I couldn't understand why, I remembered my promise to follow his lead. Sneaking a look past him, I saw what he had already noticed. A hungry heron stood at the edge of the water, searching the reeds for a likely meal. The bird towered over us, with its long, sticklike legs going on forever. Placing his finger to his lips, Frog signaled me to be silent. I nodded and followed him around the opposite edge of the pond.

We dove deep, staying out of sight near the bottom, skirting the water weeds that grew thickly on the sunny side. We were still hiding from the heron when a shadow blocked the sun. I looked up to see a large dark shape gliding through the water over our heads. A golden circle dangled from its mouth, glistening in the morning light. Suspended from the circle, little shapes twinkled in a familiar way.... It was my bracelet! I lurched forward, determined to retrieve my property, but Frog grabbed my arm and held me still until the shape had passed out of sight.

Pent-up anger and frustration propelled me to the surface when Frog finally let me go. "Did you see that?" I asked after taking a quick breath of fresh air. "That big animal—what was it?"

"An otter," replied Frog.

"It had my bracelet—the one my aunt gave me! We have to find that otter! I need that bracelet and I have to get it back!"

"No, you don't. Don't you know anything about otters?"

"Of course I do. My aunt Grassina told me all about them; where they live, how they play …"

"How they eat frogs …"

"They eat frogs?" I squeaked.

"We're their favorite food."

Suddenly, our swim didn't seem quite so carefree. I looked around, half expecting to see hungry eyes watching us from the muddy bank. "There are lots of animals that like to eat frogs, aren't there?" I asked.

Frog nodded. "We're on nearly everyone's list of favorite foods. That's why you have to be on the lookout all the time."

"And my bracelet …"

"Gone for good, which is probably just as well. You wouldn't be able to carry it now anyway. Come on, we don't have much farther to go."

A short distance later, Frog led the way up the bank and across marshy ground to a small hill. A wild plum tree grew at the top; the ground around it was littered with rotting fruit. Green and black flies zipped from one overripe plum to another.

"This is the food you were talking about?"

"Sure is. Help yourself."

Although the plums didn't look very appetizing, I was convinced that they had to taste better than the flies. I hopped to the nearest plum and tried to find a spot that wasn't too rotten.

"There's a part at the top that doesn't look bad," said Frog.

"How do I reach it from here?"

"You're a frog. Use your tongue," suggested Frog.

"My tongue? I can't do that! Are you sure I can't use my hands?"

"Not if you really want to eat. You're a frog now and frogs use their tongues."

"I don't know. I'm not very coordinated ..."

"Don't be a tadpole! You can do it!"

"I'll try," I said doubtfully. I opened my mouth and uncoiled my tongue, flicking it toward the top of the fruit. The first time I did it, I didn't put enough energy into it and my tongue flopped onto the ground.

"Nice try!" said Frog, snickering behind his hand.

I glared at him as I tried to brush the dirt and grass off my tongue. Although I was very careful, I didn't get it all off, and it felt prickly when I pulled my tongue back into my mouth. Refusing to be discouraged, I tried again with all my strength. Unfortunately, I was too enthusiastic. My tongue hit the soft skin of the rotting fruit and continued on into the center of the pulp. When I tried to pull my tongue out, it wouldn't come. I jerked my head back, hoping to yank my tongue out that way, but it just made my mouth hurt. Frog was no help at all, standing off to one side, his stomach jiggling as he laughed at me. Finally, I grabbed hold of my tongue with both hands and pulled, jerking it out so fast that it flew back and hit me in the eye. I staggered, rubbing my head while Frog rolled on the ground, holding his sides and howling.

"Thanks for the encouragement!" I said once I had my tongue back in my mouth. "I thought you said you would never laugh at me. Now what do I do?"

"Try again!" he said. "I haven't laughed this hard in a long time!"

I thought about sticking my tongue out at him, something I'd seen Violet do to one of the pageboys, but because I seemed to have so little control over it, I was afraid I might actually hit him with it by mistake. "Turn around!" I said instead. "I can't do this while you're watching me."

Frog was still chortling when he turned to face the other way. When I knew he wasn't looking, I sidled over to another piece of fruit, not liking the taste of the first plum. This one was bigger and glistened with juice. It was also covered with flies. I flicked out my tongue again, and this time I did it just right, hitting close to where I was aiming. The fruit was squishy and tasted sour, although not as bad as the first one I'd tried, but when I pulled my tongue in, a fly was stuck to the tip. It was the most disgusting thing I had ever done.

"Yuck!" I shouted. "Ged dis ding oth my tongue!" The fly wriggled and buzzed, trying to get free. Frog was there in an instant, but all he did was poke my tongue with his finger. I gagged and my tongue snapped back into place. The fly buzzed loudly, tickling the roof of my mouth.

"Mmph!" I said, pleading for help from Frog.

"Blink!" he ordered.

"Mmph?" I said again.

"Don't think, just blink!"

I couldn't imagine what blinking had to do with the fly in my mouth, but I tried it anyway. I blinked. When my eyelids closed, my eyeballs pushed down on my throat, and I swallowed the fly. I shuddered when I realized what I'd done.

"Gross! Yuck!" I said, then spit until my mouth was dry.

"Good, huh?" asked Frog.

"Good? It was disgusting!" I wiped my tongue with my fingers, trying to get rid of the taste.

"Be honest, now. What did it taste like?"

"Horrible!"

"Really?"

"Well," I said reluctantly, "the plum was sour, but the fly was kind of sweet."

"Ah-hah!" said Frog. "I knew you'd like it! You may

43

still be a princess at heart, but you're living in a frog's body, and frogs like flies!"

"I said it was sweet. I didn't say I liked it. Hey," I said, suddenly suspicious, "was this a trick? Did you bring me here so I couldn't help but catch a fly?"

"Would I do such a thing?" he asked. "Don't you know me better than that?"

"I hardly know you," I said, thinking that he might actually be a little sneaky after all.

Frog shrugged. "You couldn't go around acting all prissy and never trying anything new. You needed to see that eating a fly isn't so bad. You're going to have to get used to it if you're going to survive."

"Don't frogs eat anything other than flies?"

"Sure, lots of things. Gnats, mosquitoes, dragonflies. You name it—if it's an insect, it's on our menu."

"I'm doomed!" I moaned, but I remembered how the fly had tasted. It really hadn't been bad. Tilting my head to the side, I gave the flies an appraising look.

Frog smiled. "You ate one and it didn't kill you. Try another. It's an acquired taste, and the sooner you acquire it, the better off you'll be."

I certainly didn't intend to remain a frog my entire life, but I needed to live until I could figure out how to go back to my old self. I gagged again and swallowed hard. *Maybe,* I thought, *it would be better if I didn't think about it. Just do it and get it over with.*

"How did you learn what to do?" I asked Frog. "You couldn't have known what a frog does the instant you became one."

"I watched other frogs," Frog said, shrugging. "It's amazing what you can pick up when you're as intelligent and observant as I am. Go ahead, see if you can catch another one."

"Then go away," I told him. "It really is easier if you're not here."

Frog wandered off to catch his own meal while I looked for the juiciest plum. When I found it, I focused on the biggest fly and flicked my tongue again. It uncurled with a soundless snap, missing the fly by inches. I coiled my tongue back into my mouth while the lucky insect buzzed angrily and flew off to another, less dangerous plum. I kept trying, but I didn't catch many flies. My eye-tongue coordination wasn't very good.

Frog's stomach was full long before mine, so he came over to give me tips on improving my aim. He also came over to brag. "You should have seen what I just did!" he said. "I found a really rotten plum so covered with flies that I couldn't see the fruit. It took a while, but I lined it up just right and caught eight flies with one flick of my tongue. Eight at once! Imagine that!"

His bragging was getting on my nerves. "I have a question for you," I said, wanting to change the subject. "It was all right to call you 'Frog' when you were the only frog I knew, but now I'm a frog, too, and it no longer seems right. What should I call you?"

"You could try calling me Eadric."

"You mean you really are Prince Eadric? That wasn't something you said just to get a kiss?"

"I really was Prince Eadric, back when I was human. I'm surprised you hadn't heard of me. I was quite famous, you know. However, now that I'm a frog, I'm just plain Eadric."

"In that case, I'm Emma. Princess Emeralda is much too formal for a frog."

"Huh!" grunted Eadric. "Okay, Emma, then how about trying for that fly over there?" He pointed to an insect buzzing angrily on the ground. "Even you can catch him. I think his wing is damaged."

I ignored his suggestion, as I wanted to tell him about my idea, one I'd come up with while I stalked my flies. "I've figured out how we can get out of this mess. All we have to do is go to my castle and wait for my aunt Grassina to get home. I don't know how long she'll be gone, so we may have to wait a while, but I'm sure she'll help us as soon as she gets back."

"It's not that easy," he said as if he were talking to a simpleton.

I tried not to let him provoke me, not after he'd been trying so hard to be helpful. "Sure it is," I said. "She's a very knowledgeable witch. I'm sure she'll know what to do."

"That's not what I mean. In the first place, waiting around a castle would be an invitation for disaster. Frogs aren't exactly welcome on castle grounds. Don't you think I would have gone home if I could have? I've seen too many frogs tortured by dogs, cats, and bored under-gardeners. It's something I'd rather not experience, thank you very much! And although I don't really know all that much about magic, even I understand that one witch can't undo spells cast by another. In fact, adding a second witch's magic would only make the spell that much harder to undo. Your aunt wouldn't be the one to see. We'd have to go to the witch who cast the spell in the first place. In cases like this, it's always best to go to the source."

"Then let's go see her!"

"I don't know where she lives."

"You aren't very encouraging," I said, trying not to show how discouraged I actually felt. "Maybe Grassina could help us find her—"

"Hold it right there. Didn't you hear a word I just said? I don't want to sit around your castle waiting for your aunt to show up! Anyway, I *am not* going to go talk to any strange witch. How do I know she won't cast another spell on me?"

"My aunt wouldn't do anything like that."

"Really? Then tell me, has she ever turned anyone into a frog? Be honest now."

"Well, yes, but—"

"Ah-hah! And you wanted me to go see her! It'll be a cold day in the swamp before I go see another spell-casting witch!"

"But she's not—"

"Forget it!" Eadric said, turning his back to me. "There's nothing you can say that would change my mind."

I sighed. I'd met stubborn people before, but none of them had been as aggravating as this frog!

"So what do we do now?" I asked, thinking fondly of my aunt Grassina's rooms, where I often headed at the end of the day.

"Let's go back to my pad," said Eadric. "I want to show you my collection."

"Your collection?" I wondered what a frog could possibly collect.

"My dragonfly wings, remember?"

"Oh, right," I said. He was the strangest prince I'd ever met. Of course, if I were to remain a frog for as long as he had, I might seem awfully strange, too. The thought was depressing, considering how many people already regarded me as odd. There was only one solution: I was going to have to get myself turned back as quickly as possible.

Six

Daylight was fading as Eadric escorted me to his lily pad, which was tucked in a quiet backwater of the stream. It was a large, smooth pad, floating near the overhanging branches of a weeping willow. I tried to climb onto it, but it kept sagging under me, dumping me back into the water. After I'd tried three or four times, Eadric got impatient and shoved me onto it from behind. He pushed me so hard that I skidded across the pad, nearly sliding off the other side. When I tried to climb to my feet, the lousy thing dipped and swayed and I slipped helplessly.

"Isn't it great!" enthused Eadric as he strode to the middle of his pad. "That willow is so close that some days I don't even have to go anywhere to eat. It's almost always full of bugs and I can catch them without even trying. I can even do it lying down. See that spider dangling from the end of that leaf? Watch this!" Stretching out on his side, Eadric rested his chin in his hand and flicked out his tongue, plucking the spider from the leaf like an expert.

"How convenient," I said, certain that he couldn't get any lazier.

Nee deep! Nee deep! We were interrupted by deep voices sounding from the undergrowth lining the stream bank. *Pa reep! Pa reep!* Higher-pitched voices from among the trees joined in the chorus.

"What is that?" I asked.

"Just some of my friends. They have concerts every night this time of year, as long as the weather is nice."

"You have friends among the common frogs? I'm happy to hear that you're not a snob like Jorge!"

Eadric scowled at me and shook his head. "There is no royalty in the animal kingdom. All frogs are created equal. My friends are a great bunch of guys. I'll introduce you to them after the concert. Let's go. I know where we can get good seats if we hurry."

We slipped off the lily pad into the water and swam side by side to the soft mud of the stream bank. Frogs of every size had already begun to gather at the edge of the water. "That's Bassey over there," Eadric said, pointing to a large frog whose deep voice resonated throughout the crowd. "And that little guy is Peepers. He's a soprano." The little frog saw Eadric and waved from his vantage point on a tree.

Eadric led me to a soft patch of grass, picking his

way between the frogs who had already taken their seats. A few frogs greeted us while others smiled their welcome, making me feel comfortable from the start.

"This is nice," I said, settling down beside Eadric.

He bent down and spoke directly into my eardrum. "I'm glad you like it. So how about a kiss now?"

"Eadric!" I said so loudly that everyone turned to stare. There'd been a pause in the music, making my voice sound that much louder. Embarrassed, I waited until the music resumed. "I can't kiss you now! All your friends are watching!"

"It's all right," he said. "We'll close our eyes."

"No, thank you. I don't want to take any chances. No more kisses until we know why the first one went wrong!" I was too loud again, and the frogs seated closest to us turned around to shush me. Covering my face with my hands, I shrank into my seat, almost wishing we hadn't come.

More frogs arrived, joining in the chorus. I was surprised when Eadric began to sing, too. I liked his voice, which wasn't as deep as Bassey's or as high as Peeper's. *I could listen to this all night,* I thought, closing my eyes. The warm evening breeze felt good on my skin. The music was so beautiful that it gave me chills down my spine and frog bumps on my arms.

Nee deep, nee deep! sang the big frogs like Bassey. *Pa reep, pa reep!* sang the tiny frogs like Peepers. *Barbidy,*

51

barbidy! sang Eadric. I was nodding my head in time to the music when suddenly the night grew silent and I opened my eyes to see why. A grass snake as long as a human man's arm slithered out of the weeds edging the stream. Before anyone could move, the snake struck, sinking its fangs into a member of the audience. The poor frog was halfway down the snake's gullet in an instant. Its twitching legs stuck out of the snake's mouth, kicking and jerking as if the frog could still hop away and escape. It was horrible! I screamed and the snake swiveled its head to look directly into my eyes.

"Come on!" urged Eadric, squeezing my arm to get my attention. Mesmerized by the snake's eyes, I couldn't move. "I said, come on!" Eadric shouted again, yanking my arm until I turned away. "Jump!" he yelled as the snake slithered toward me.

I jumped, landing on the back of an old frog crawling through the shallow water. "Sorry!" I said. "I didn't mean—"

"Hurry up!" shouted Eadric, from the middle of the stream. "You don't have time to apologize!"

"Sorry!" I said again, and pushed off from a slippery rock, sailing into the air and landing far out in the stream. "I can't do this!" I screamed, spluttering as I got a mouthful of water. "I can't live this way!"

"Don't think, swim!" he shouted, pulling me.

With Eadric at my side, I scissor-kicked as fast as I

could until I was too tired to kick any longer. Eadric found a place to hide in a mud bank far downstream. Guiding me to the hole, he helped me climb inside.

I was terrified and couldn't stop shaking. Eadric patted my back consolingly. "It's all right," he said. "That snake can't find us here."

"But there are other snakes!" I whispered, my throat tight with fear. "Sooner or later one is going to get us! I can't live like this, Eadric. I was never afraid that I would be eaten when I was a princess. You must know someone who can help us!"

"There is one possibility," Eadric said reluctantly. "It's sort of a last resort, but we can try it if you really want to."

"What are you talking about?"

"We can go see the old witch who turned me into a frog. I don't know where she lives, but each month on the night of the full moon she goes to a certain spot to collect plants—or at least she used to. The full moon is only two nights away. We can reach it in time if we leave in the morning."

"Do you really think she'd help us?"

"She might. She said I just needed to be kissed by a princess to become a prince again. You're a princess and you kissed me, so why am I still a frog? The old witch cast the spell, so she's responsible for making sure it works. She should know how to fix it."

"Why didn't you tell me about this before? You knew I didn't want to be a frog!"

"Because it's risky. There's no telling if she'll help or not or even if she'll be there. Besides," he said, blushing a dark green, "if I have to remain a frog, it's kind of nice having another frog around who once was a human. I enjoy your company. But," he added briskly, "we'll do it if you really want to."

"Oh, believe me, I do! I don't think I could stand being a frog for much longer!"

I didn't know what to think of Eadric's confession. He could be rude and obnoxious, but underneath it all he was a nice frog and I liked him. Even so ... I went to sleep that night thinking about Eadric. Considerate and helpful, he treated me as if I were an important person worthy of his attention. And it was much more pleasant to think about him than it was to think about that horrid snake and the poor little frog that had been eaten.

I'd been asleep only a short time when something woke me. I looked around, but nothing had changed inside the hole and Eadric was snoring peacefully beside me. Then it came again, the mournful sound of a dog howling in the distance. Instead of frightening me, I felt sorry for the beast, since I felt like howling myself. *But it's luckier than I am,* I thought. *At least it doesn't have to worry about being eaten.* I shivered and moved closer to Eadric, safe for the moment in our muddy sanctuary.

Seven

Eadric and I woke long before the sun was up the next morning. Even though I wasn't hungry, Eadric insisted that we have our breakfast before setting out. It was still dark and there were plenty of mosquitoes around. I was surprised when I tasted my first one. It was salty, but extremely filling for such a skinny insect.

"We'll be traveling over land for the first part of our trip," explained Eadric between mosquitoes. "We'll be safe enough as long as we follow some rules. One, don't make any unnecessary noise. Two, eat while you hop—we're on a tight schedule. Three, keep your eyes and eardrums open at all times. If you hear anything suspicious, don't talk. Just signal me like this." Eadric flapped his arm and patted his head. "That should get my attention."

"Yours and that of every other creature around," I said. "What if I tap you on the shoulder instead?"

"Fine," Eadric said, nodding. "That should work, too."

Our trip began over swampy ground, but as the sun rose overhead, we reached higher, drier land. I stopped to admire a bedraggled patch of dandelions, having had little contact with flowers other than the crystalline blossoms in Grassina's room. Ordinary flowers were banned from the castle because both my mother and my aunt were allergic to them.

I continued on when Eadric harrumphed impatiently, and we soon found ourselves hopping across pebbled earth where little seemed to grow. It made us both nervous, for the rocky soil and occasional scraggly weeds gave us nothing to hide behind if a predator should come along. Eadric and I hurried across the open ground, anxious to reach the tall grass beyond it. Suddenly, a ladybug zipped past my nose and flew toward a short, squat rock. I remembered Eadric's advice to eat while we hopped and tried to do just that. I jumped, flicking out my tongue at the same time, but the target was smaller than I was used to and I missed, my tongue coming back empty. Since I'd been concentrating on my tongue, I hadn't been paying attention to my feet, so I tripped and fell flat on my face. *Thppt!* Someone else's tongue flicked out and caught the ladybug.

"Better luck next time," said a gravelly voice. I stared

in disbelief. What looked like a rock blinked and shifted a lumpy foot.

"You're a toad!" I exclaimed, startled.

"And you're a lousy jumper!" replied the toad. "Just how old are you, anyway?"

"What does that have to do with anything?" I asked.

"I haven't seen such lousy jumping since my tadpoles first got their legs!" replied the toad. "You're going to have to work on your coordination if you're going to catch anything."

"She's been a frog only for a few days," said Eadric.

"What was she before that?" asked the toad.

"I can speak for myself, thank you." I said. "I was a princess!"

"That explains it. Never have seen a princess who could jump worth grasshopper spit. Whoa!" said the toad, looking behind me. "Look out, little lady. Here comes a big one."

I turned around, expecting to see a large insect. Instead, the same huge white dog that had once tried to eat me was trotting straight toward us. I couldn't take my eyes off it.

"You might want to sidle on out of the way," suggested the toad. "I can handle this one."

I scurried behind a scraggly clump of grass while the toad hopped boldly into the open. After one look at my face, the toad laughed. "Don't worry, little lady, I know how to take care of myself. Watch this!"

Three more hops set the toad directly in the dog's path. The dog's eyes lit up. "Hmmm!" it said, snuffling the toad from front to back before closing its great jaws around the lumpy, gray body. A strange look came over the dog's face and it dropped the toad as if it were hot. White foam dripped from between the dog's jaws. Whimpering pitifully, it pawed at its mouth.

"Yuck!" said the dog. "What *is* this stuff?" It shook its head and great flecks of foam splattered the dry soil. With a pained yelp, the dog ran back the way it had come.

"You poor thing! Are you all right?" I asked the toad.

"Fine as frog's hair. Thanks for asking."

"What did you do?" I asked. "I thought it had you!"

"Not me! Mother Nature gave us toads a little secret weapon." The toad lowered his voice to a conspiratorial whisper. "You frogs think you're so superior with your smooth skin and your pretty faces, but you don't have anything like this. You see back here behind my head? This gooey stuff isn't dog spit, no sirree! I make my own poison and I've been told it tastes downright nasty. Heh, heh, heh! That dog didn't stand a chance."

"That poison … He isn't seriously hurt, is he?"

"Nah, nothing time won't cure. Might have learned a lesson, though, if he's lucky."

"I never would have guessed that you could do that."

"That's what makes it a secret weapon!" the toad

said. He beamed at me before turning to Eadric. Eadric scowled back.

"We'd better be going," I said. "Thanks for your help!"

"My pleasure, little lady. Good luck with your hopping! Keep on practicing and you'll do just fine."

Eadric and I continued on, neither of us saying another word until we were concealed by a tall, rippling sea of grass. Once we were in its shade, I breathed a sigh of relief. "Now what was that all about?" I asked Eadric. "I think this was the first time I've seen you looking angry."

"He didn't have to do that!" grumbled Eadric.

"What do you mean?" I asked. "Who didn't have to do what?"

"That old toad. He didn't have to show off like that! Who does he think he is, your knight in warty armor? If anybody is going to rescue you, it will be me! We didn't need him! If he hadn't interfered, I would have done something about that dog."

"Like what?"

"I don't know. Something would have occurred to me, I'm sure. But I didn't need some old toad to protect you like that. Interfering old busybody!"

"Eadric, he was just trying to be helpful."

"We didn't need his help! Look at me! I'm big! I'm strong! I'm a superior example of froghood and capable

59

of protecting us both!"

I gave up. From the furious scowl on Eadric's face, I was better off not saying anything.

Intent on maneuvering through the dense grass, I ignored my companion. Because there were few clear areas that allowed straightforward hopping, I had to develop my own crawl-hop-wiggle style that got me through the grass but left my muscles aching.

The stars were twinkling overhead when Eadric and I finally reached the edge of the grassy field and took shelter under a flowering thornbush.

The next morning, we entered a trembling copse of young saplings and heard the distant murmur of rushing water. With the sound as our guide, we detoured around boulders and old stumps, breathing a sigh of relief when the tangled underbrush bordering the stream came into sight. We had been out of the water for so long that my throat was parched and my skin was beginning to feel like old leather. Working my way through the maze of stems and branches, I leaped into the clear, sun-sparkled water only seconds ahead of Eadric.

The swim was easy and relaxing, because we were heading downstream. I swam beside Eadric, kicking now and then but mostly letting the current do the work. Around midday, fat black clouds gathered overhead. Rain peppered the water, landing on my head in oversized, heavy drops. *A little more water won't hurt us,* I thought, but at the first crack of thunder, I began to feel uneasy.

"How much farther is it?" I asked Eadric, who had been single-mindedly looking for landmarks.

"We're closer than I thought. Do you see that old oak over there?" Eadric pointed to a tree on the far side of the stream. "I tied my horse to the lowest branch the night I was turned into a frog. I wonder what became of him. His name was Bright Country and he was the best horse I'd ever had. I'd hate to think that something bad happened to the old fellow."

"I'm sure someone found him or he got himself loose. I don't see any old horse bones lying there. But why did you come here? You've never told me the story."

"It was no epic tale, believe me. I thought I was in love with a princess and hoped to win her favor by giving her some meadwort. I'd heard that if you picked it at midnight on the night of the full moon, then boiled the leaves, you could see your true love's face in the bottom of your cup. I was convinced that I was her true love and that it was my face she'd see."

"I've never heard so much garbage! Meadwort doesn't do anything like that. Who told you that it did?"

"My little brother," Eadric admitted.

"And you believed him? I don't know much about little brothers, but from what I've heard they are not the most reliable sources of information. It sounds like he pulled one over on you."

"I guess so."

Eadric's face looked so forlorn that I took pity on him. "I'm sure he wouldn't have done it if he'd known how it would end."

"Probably not," admitted Eadric. "He isn't a bad sort."

"I didn't know you were a romantic at heart."

"Romantic! Is that what you call it? I thought I was just having a run of bad luck. The really sad part is that a few months after I became a frog, I saw the princess. Her coach almost ran over me when I was crossing the road. It was decorated for a wedding, so it must have been her wedding day. My rival won by default, I guess. She'd been seeing a lot of him while I'd still been a human. That's why I'd even considered my brother's advice. I was getting desperate."

"You didn't finish your story. What happened when you came looking for the meadwort?"

"I never found it, but I did come across the old witch. She was out looking for plants that night, too. I stumbled across her in the dark, which was pretty unpleasant, believe me. She was wearing a filthy gown and smelled terrible. That's when I made a comment about her clothes and hygiene. She took offense and wham! The prince became a frog!"

"So how much farther is it?"

"It's right there," said Eadric. "We can wait under that blackberry bush. That's where I spent my first night as a frog. If there are any rotten berries on the ground, we should find plenty of insects."

Eadric and I climbed out of the water and made ourselves comfortable under the blackberry bush. To our disappointment, we found neither berries nor insects, although the leaves kept the cold rain off us. It had been a long, tiring trip and we hadn't slept well in days. With the soothing patter of rain on the leaves, it wasn't long before we were both asleep.

Eight

When we woke, the rain had stopped and the air felt clean and cool. The full moon peered through a gap in the clouds, casting an otherworldly light on the landscape. We spoke in soft whispers, not wishing to disturb the silence that comes after a heavy rain.

"Is it almost midnight?" I asked.

"I don't know," said Eadric, "but it must be getting close."

"Thank you."

"What for?"

"For bringing me here when you really didn't want to. I know how you feel about seeing the old witch again, but you said you'd help me and you have. Thank you."

"You're welcome. You know, of course, that my motives are not completely unselfish. I want to be turned back into a human, too. Even so, I know of a way you could thank me."

"And what's that?" I asked, certain I already knew the answer.

"You could kiss me." He puckered his lips and stretched his neck to bring his head close to mine.

"At a time like this? The witch could be here any moment!"

"But I don't want to kiss her!" said Eadric.

"I didn't—"

"Listen," said Eadric. "I think I hear something."

It came again. Someone was approaching and making no effort to be quiet.

"Look! That must be her," whispered Eadric. A light bobbed across the uneven ground. The sound of footsteps slogging through the muck could be clearly heard in the still night air.

As the witch approached, the full moon outlined her silhouette, yet did little to illuminate her face. The light of the lantern she carried had been focused toward the ground by the use of movable shutters, leaving her face in relative darkness. Indistinctly seen in the moonlight, the woman resembled a ghostly apparition. Her wild, uncombed hair hung loosely about her shoulders. She wore long, dark garments that dragged on the ground, snagging twigs and muck as she walked.

Trying to get up the courage to approach her, Eadric and I cowered under the berry bush. The witch drew near, intent on her midnight search.

"Hurry," I told him. "She'll be gone and we'll have lost our chance."

"I'm not sure I should," said Eadric. "I have a bad feeling about this. Our last meeting didn't end very well."

"Please go. It's why we're here," I said. "I'll go with you. Just be nice and discreet this time. Remember, no sarcastic comments!"

"Fine, if you'll stop making up rules—it'll be hard enough as it is." Together we hopped into the witch's path. When the light of the lantern reached us, we covered our eyes against the glare.

"Ma'am," called Eadric. "We need to talk to you. It's urgent!"

The witch stopped short and set the lantern on the ground.

"You might remember me. I'm Prince Eadric," he said warily, trying to see the witch past the brilliance of the light. "We met here one night and had a short conversation. I said something about your sense of style and you turned me into a frog."

"Go on," said the witch.

"You said I'd stay a frog until a princess kissed me, but I did and nothing happened. You have to do something!"

"What do you mean nothing happened?" I exclaimed. "I turned into a frog, too! I think that's a pretty big something!"

"This is Princess Emeralda. She's the one who kissed me."

"This wasn't supposed to happen!" I said. "You must

66

have done something wrong when you cast the spell."

"Shh! Emma!" whispered Eadric. "Don't make her mad! And you told me to be discreet!"

"But I—"

Eadric cleared his throat and turned back to the witch. "We didn't come to accuse anyone of anything. We just need your help fixing it."

"Really? And how would I do that?" the witch asked in a friendly voice.

Encouraged, I couldn't keep the words from tumbling out. "Just turn us back into humans and I'll see that you're handsomely rewarded. My parents will do anything to get me back."

"Is that so? And I'm the lucky witch you chose to talk to! My, oh, my," she said, her voice losing its sweet tone. "You picked the wrong one tonight, froggies! Or should I call you Your Royal Highnesses?" In one swift motion, the woman dropped the sack she'd been carrying and swooped down on us, snatching us off the ground and raising us to eye level. She studied us intently, turning us over and examining us from top to bottom. "Such nice, strong specimens! You two will do just fine."

For the first time we could see the woman's face. She was young. Her long, frizzy hair had been dyed black and showed mouse-brown roots. Her eyes were dark and sunken, her cheeks gaunt, and her skin pale. Everything she wore was black, from her long, threadbare dress and ratty shawl to her worn leather shoes.

"Emma," Eadric whispered in a horrified voice, "it's not her! This isn't the witch who did it!"

"You are a smart froggy, aren't you, Prince? I've never turned anyone into a frog, but I've been looking for two frogs like you. Your bad luck is my good fortune! Two talking frogs in one night. My luck has finally changed." The witch hummed happily as she opened the sack and dropped us in.

I landed on my back. Wiggling and twisting, I tried to turn myself over. It was dark inside the sack, with an overwhelming musty smell. I scrabbled for a handhold on the coarse cloth, wishing I had my bracelet with me. Even the small amount of light it gave off would have been helpful. A moment later the woman lifted the sack and we tumbled to the bottom, where we lay in a tangled heap.

"Ow!" moaned Eadric, rubbing the side of his head. "Watch your elbow, will you?"

"Sorry," I said, "but I didn't hit you on purpose. Maybe if we sat up …"

I kicked the sack, the weight of our bodies making the fabric taut, but my leg bounced off and caught Eadric squarely in the stomach.

"Oof," he said, doubling over.

"Sorry," I said again. "Are you all right?"

I'd knocked the breath out of him, so it took a moment for him to answer. When he did, he was wheezing and I felt awful. "I'll be just fine ... if you'll hold still!" he said.

I inched away, trying to put some space between us, but being inside a sack didn't make it easy.

The sack began to move, swaying like a pendulum with each of the witch's steps. As she walked, she muttered to herself in a voice too low for me to understand. Suddenly, she stopped and set the sack roughly on the ground. Eadric and I could hear her trudge away, although she didn't go far.

"Quick!" I said. "See if you can open the top of the bag. Maybe we can get out while she's gone."

Eadric shifted his weight beside me. I tensed, trying to keep out of his way while he reached toward the top of the sack. "It's no use," he said a moment later. "She's tied the top shut."

"Never mind. The way our luck has been running, she'll probably be back soon anyway. Can you believe that witch? She doesn't care who we are. It looks like we're more valuable to her as talking frogs than we are as royalty. What are we going to do, Eadric?"

"I really am sorry about this," began Eadric. "If I hadn't tried to get you to kiss me ..."

"I never would have met the best friend I've ever had. You're not the only one responsible for this. No one made me kiss you. And if it weren't for me, we wouldn't have come out here to talk with the witch. So stop feeling guilty and help me figure out a way to get through this."

"Maybe if we move to the opposite sides of the bag ..."

"We'll roll together again like we did last time. At least if we start out near each other we won't bump together as hard when she picks up the sack."

"I have an even better idea," said Eadric. "If I hold on to you, we won't roll into each other at all."

"Fine," I said. "We could try that."

"And while I'm there, you might as well give me a kiss."

"What?"

"Who knows what that witch has in mind? She might toss us in a cauldron of boiling water or feed us to a pet dragon. This may be our last chance to show how we feel about each other."

"Show how we ... Are you crazy? Kissing you is the last thing I want to do right now!"

"Hey, it sounded like a good idea to me."

"I told you," I said, getting exasperated, "I don't want to take any chances!"

I could feel the ground vibrate as the witch returned. She opened the sack suddenly and the moonlight poured in.

"Do you think we could make a run for it?" I whispered in Eadric's eardrum. "Because if she—"

A small, thorn-covered plant fell on us. The wet mud encasing the roots dripped in sour-smelling globs onto our heads. Sputtering, I covered my face with my hands.

"Ow!" wailed Eadric. "Those thorns are sharp!"

I spit out a mouthful of mud. "Try not to talk. That stuff tastes terrible!"

The witch jerked the sack off the ground and carried it a few yards. She opened the top again, but only long enough to drop in a handful of leaves. I cringed, having recognized the shape of the poison oak leaf at once, but it was too late and I knew it. *I'm in for it now,* I thought. Even the briefest contact with poison oak gave me a rash, and now my back was covered with the leaves.

When the witch picked up the sack, Eadric and I tensed our muscles, waiting for the next impact with the ground. But the sack continued to sway in the witch's hands as she slogged across the marshy ground. After a while, Eadric began to groan.

"What's wrong?" I asked. "Is it the thorns?"

"No," whispered Eadric.

"Is it the mud?"

"No," whispered Eadric.

"Then what is it?"

"It's this swaying back and forth," he said. "I don't feel very well."

"Take a deep breath and think of something else. And please face the other way if you're going to be sick."

If the witch's house had been any farther, we might not have made it. As it was, Eadric was groaning loudly long before the witch opened her cottage door and I was worried that he wasn't going to survive the trip: he was groaning so much that if he didn't die of bag-sickness first, I was going to strangle him to put him out of his misery. I wondered if all male frogs were such babies when they were sick, or only the ones who used to be princes.

I was still trying to block out Eadric's moans by covering my eardrums with my hands when the witch set her lantern down with a clang. Reaching into the sack, she grabbed us and shoved us into a small wicker cage. My head spinning, I lay on the cage floor while she slammed the door shut and fastened a complicated latch.

"There," she said. "That should hold you until I'm ready."

"Ready for what?" I asked the witch as my head cleared. The woman ignored me and emptied her sack onto a rickety table in the middle of the room.

"Yoo-hoo, Witchy! Ready for what?" Eadric echoed me in a shaky voice. The witch turned her back on our cage and took off her shawl.

"Has anyone ever told you that you're very rude?" Eadric asked, his voice getting stronger. "You kidnap us, lock us in a cage without an explanation, and expect us to be nice, well-behaved frogs. Obviously, you don't know me. I don't take anything quietly!"

"Eadric! Shh!" I hissed at him. "You'll make things worse!"

"How can it get worse than this? We were better off as free frogs happily living in the swamp. Now we're stuck here with Rudella the witch and we don't even know why. Hey, Witchy! Answer me! What do you want with us?"

When the witch continued to ignore him, Eadric got a funny look in his eyes. "No witch is going to ignore me for long," he whispered in my eardrum. "Watch this!" He thought for a minute, then planted his hands firmly on his middle and called out, "Hey, Witchy! You're so ugly that you don't have to dye your clothes! One look at you and they die on their own!"

I could see the witch's back stiffen, but that wasn't enough for Eadric. He winked at me, then shouted, "I know why you don't have any mirrors in this place. You got tired of cleaning up the broken glass!"

With a cry of rage, the witch whirled around, scowling ferociously. "Listen, Your Royal Lowness, I don't like frogs and I like princes even less! I suggest you keep your rubbery little lips shut if you ever want to see the light of day again. Now lock those lips, sit down, and don't move. I'll be right back!" Taking a small vial from a shelf, the witch stomped out the door.

"You couldn't be quiet, could you?" I asked. "If that was the kind of thing you said to the other witch, it's no wonder she turned you into a frog! And now you've gotten a second witch mad at you. Who knows what she's going to do."

"She doesn't care what I say. What can we do? We're in a cage, for frog's sake! If we annoy her enough, maybe she'll let us go."

"Or kill us so she doesn't have to listen to you," I said.

Eadric and I were glowering at each other when the witch returned with a freshly unearthed nightcrawler in her hand. With a gleam in her eye, she dropped the dirt-flecked worm through the bars of our cage and set the vial back on the shelf.

"There you go!" she said in a syrupy voice. "Have a bedtime snack. Get some sleep and don't worry so much. Too much stress can make you sick and we don't want that, now, do we?" With that, the witch blew out the lantern and shuffled across the room.

Tiptoeing to the side of the cage, I listened as the witch kicked off her shoes and settled back on an old straw-filled mattress. Seconds later her breathing evened out in sleep.

"Do you want some?" Eadric said through a mouthful of worm.

I spun around in surprise. "What are you doing? I thought you were sick to your stomach. You shouldn't eat any of that—it might be poisoned! Spit it out! Spit it out right now!"

"Are you kidding? This is delicious. It's not poisoned. Here, try some."

"Great," I said. "I'm stuck in a cage with an idiot who eats food given to him by a witch and will probably be dead by morning."

"Hey, I'm not the one who's going to bed hungry. You are such a worrier! I've eaten half of this worm already and I still feel fine. If you're sure you don't want any, I'm going to finish the worm and get some sleep. We'll think of a way to get out of this in the morning. Now, leave me alone and let me enjoy my worm in peace. Unlike someone else around here, I know how to appreciate the finer things in life."

Furious, I went to the back of the cage, as far from Eadric as I could get, and tried to shut out the sound of munching. Although Eadric was soon asleep, I was too restless to lie down. I paced the width of the cage, the gritty floor crunching beneath my feet, but I couldn't sleep and I couldn't come up with an escape plan, either.

After a while I stopped talking to myself and listened to the sounds of the night. I'd heard something stirring at the other end of the room, a dry rustle that could have been caused by just about anything. Then something else moved overhead until it seemed to be right above me. Whatever else was in the room, I wasn't the only one who was awake. Suddenly, I had something else to make me nervous. Not knowing who or what might be there, I hunched down in the middle of the cage, hoping that the bars were as effective at keeping creatures out as they were at keeping us in. When I finally drifted off to sleep, it was to dreams of my family's dungeon and large, frog-eating worms that made me itch when they touched me.

Nine

It was the itching that woke me the next morning. The rash that I'd predicted the night before covered my back, and no matter how I twisted or turned, I couldn't reach all the itchy spots. I was getting desperate when I finally found that if I twisted around a certain way and rubbed against a bar of the cage, I could relieve some of the worst itching.

"You look like an old bear when you do that," said a voice from above. "Not that I've seen many old bears."

A bright shaft of sunlight came through a hole high on the wall, in the general direction from which the voice had come. At first I thought I might be having a divine visitation, but the voice had been high and squeaky, not at all the sort of voice I thought would belong to a divine being. *Maybe it's a trick,* I thought. But it couldn't be Eadric. He was still sound asleep. It wasn't the witch, either. I could see her lying on her back with her head turned to the side. Her mouth was open, drool trickling onto the thin mattress with the stained gray cover.

"Where are you?" I asked, squinting through the shaft of sunlight and the dancing dust motes. Other than the cracks in the shutters covering the two windows, the hole in the wall was the only source of light in the room.

"I'm up here," squeaked the voice. "By the rafters."

I looked toward the ceiling. A tiny patch of darkness seemed to shift, but I couldn't be sure. "Sorry," I said. "I can't really make you out from here...."

"But I'm right ... oh, forget it. Here, is this better?"

A bit of shadow detached itself from the rafter and flapped down into the dimly lit room. "Oh, my," I said, taken by surprise. It was a bat. As a rule, I didn't like bats, although I'd never encountered one in person before. It was just that I'd heard so many bad things about them.

"Are you satisfied yet? Can I go back to my rafter now?" the bat asked.

"Of course!" I said, embarrassed by my bad manners. "I didn't mean to inconvenience you."

"Inconvenience! My, aren't you a nice little frog! None of the other idiots around here would ever think about what is or isn't convenient for me. Take that nasty little witch on the bed, for instance."

I turned toward the witch in the back of the room, afraid that she might be awake and listening. "Don't worry," said the bat. "Vannabe's still asleep. I always know when she's awake, believe me. Anyway, she never thinks about what's convenient for me. It's always 'Go away, ya stupid bat!' or 'Get that bug, ya stupid bat!' If I didn't know better, I'd think my name was Stupid Bat. It isn't, of course. It's Li'l Stinker. That's what my first mistress named me when I was a youngster. Now, that woman was far more considerate. She used to say, 'Li'l Stinker, you'd better get that fat, juicy bug or you won't have any dinner tonight.' See what I mean? She was a much more thoughtful person."

I was beginning to feel overwhelmed. I had always thought that bats were quiet creatures, but this bat could talk more than anyone I'd ever met.

I rubbed my back against the bar again. The rash was itching more now and was spreading to my chest.

"I couldn't help but hear you talking to Vannabe last night," said Li'l. "You can talk to humans, huh? That's too bad. The only humans I can talk to are witches with the talent and that's the way I like it. So, did your friend eat the worm?"

"He sure did. He ate the whole thing. I was afraid that he'd be poisoned, but he's fine."

"I wouldn't say that exactly. He's still asleep, isn't he?"

"Well, yes, but neither of us has gotten much sleep lately. He's really tired."

"Is that it? Go shake him and wake him up."

"I was going to let him sleep for a while. He needs his rest."

"Go shake him now and see what he does."

"I'd rather not."

"Just do it! It's for your own good!"

It was obvious that the bossy little bat was going to pester me until I did what she'd said. Reluctantly, I hopped to Eadric's side and gently shook his shoulder. He continued to snore. I shook him harder. He snorted and rolled over.

"I can't seem to wake him," I said, frowning.

"Of course not. You won't be able to if he ate that worm! Didn't you see that vial Vannabe had in her hand? It was sleeping potion. A tiny drop and you'll sleep for days. What do you think those witches used to help Sleeping Beauty and Snow White get all that beauty rest? A full vial can knock you out for a hundred years or more. Now, unless you want to take a very long nap, I suggest that you don't let the witch know that you're still awake. Go curl up somewhere and pretend that you're asleep or she'll find another way to give you that potion. She has her reasons for wanting you two to stay quiet. Now watch out!" Li'l Stinker said softly. "She's waking up."

I scurried to the back of the cage and pretended to be asleep, just in case the bat was right. With my eyes half closed, I watched Vannabe yawn, sit up, and scratch her ribs. Drool shone wetly on her cheek, but she didn't seem to notice. Kicking off the grimy blanket, she swung her feet to the floor.

"What are you looking at?" Vannabe said grumpily, looking up at the bat. Li'l Stinker didn't give her an answer, but the witch obviously didn't expect one, for she stood up and shuffled across the room without another word.

Still in her bare feet, Vannabe went out the door, leaving it open. I thought the fresh air would be a relief, but instead it stirred up the dust in the room and recirculated the odor of unwashed clothes, filthy cages, bat droppings, and old grease. I was almost happy to see the witch come back inside and close the door behind her.

Still scratching her ribs, Vannabe shuffled to the fireplace, where she bent over the fire, her back to our cage. She lifted a wooden spoon from a hook on the wall and stirred something in a greasy black pot. Then she took it to the table in the middle of the room and sat down to eat. When she was finished, she scraped the bottom of the pot with her wooden spoon.

"Here now, can't have anyone go hungry with all this good food around, can we?" said the witch as she walked toward our side of the room. "Don't eat it all at once, 'cause you won't be getting any more today."

My view was blocked by a stack of books on one side and a collection of bottles on the other, but I could hear other creatures moving about in their cages as the witch gave each of them their own dollop of food.

When the witch came near our cage, I kept my eyes closed and made my breath come slowly and evenly, trying to make it sound like Eadric's. Vannabe opened the cage door and I thought my heart would beat its way out of my chest, but I willed myself to hold still. Even when a long fingernail poked me in the ribs, I kept my eyes closed and stayed as limp as I could. "Princess, huh?" Vannabe's voice was harsh and mocking. "What's it like being a frog, Miss High and Mighty?"

The hand moved away and I refused to look, picturing Eadric receiving the same treatment. "As for you, Prince ... slain any dragons lately, or is it dragonflies now?" Vannabe laughed, the shrill sound grating on my eardrums. *And people say that I have a strange laugh,* I thought.

When the cage door had shut with a soft click and I was sure that the witch had moved away, I opened my eyes to slits and was relieved to see her pick up her sack from the floor and head out the door. "Behave yourselves, vermin!" she told the animals. "No wild parties while I'm gone!" Laughing, the witch slammed the door behind her.

With the witch gone, I could finally relax. I bent my leg and scratched my back with my toe, but I still couldn't reach the really itchy spots.

For the first time I was able to take a better look at my surroundings. The cottage was small, with the witch's bed against the wall opposite the only door. Li'l Stinker hung from a rough-hewn rafter near the front of the cottage and appeared to be asleep. Birds' bones suspended from a frayed cord clattered together. Our cage rested on a dust-covered shelf next to a stack of books. The skull of an unborn baby dragon sat on top of the books, the dust so thick that the eye sockets were nearly filled.

A collection of jars and bottles stood on the other side of the cage. They were all labeled, although some of the labels were turned so that I couldn't read them. Rabbits' ears, cats' tails, and wild boars' tusks filled some of the larger jars, and crystals and dried compounds filled others. One jar was filled with dark blue, fuzzy clumps and was labeled *Troll Navel Lint.* Another contained smooth white balls suspended in a clear liquid. When one bobbed about, turning to stare at me, I gasped: they were eyeballs, obviously alive, from the way they jostled for position. I quickly realized that there were other jars with living contents, like the squirming, puckering pieces of green flesh in a jar labeled *Lizard Lip*s and the wrinkled, snuffling *Pig Snouts.* The contents of one slim vial may not have been alive, but the colored gases swirled, mixing and separating in intricate, never-repeating patterns.

Something thumped by the fireplace and I scurried across my cage to look. There was nothing there but an old stick used for poking logs and two crudely constructed barrels, one labeled *Trash Can,* the other *Trash Can't.* The Trash Can was uncovered. When I listened carefully, I thought I could hear something gurgling inside. A wooden lid covered the Trash Can't and as I watched, I could see the whole thing shake and thump. To my surprise, I could also hear creatures calling from other cages.

"Who are they?" squeaked one voice.

"I don't know, but I heard one of them talking to Li'l Stinker." The speaker's voice was so faint and breathy that I had to strain to hear it.

"Do you think she'll introduce us?"

"I don't know. Ask Miss Bossy. You know she always has to be in charge."

"I'd be happy to," interrupted the bat. "But I don't know their names yet. Hey there, Frog!"

Because I'd heard the entire conversation, I was ready when Li'l called to me. "I'm Emma and this is Eadric," I began. "We're both enchanted frogs. I'm a princess and Eadric is really a prince."

I had never heard animals howl with laughter before. It would have made me feel defensive if they hadn't sounded so funny. I began to laugh, too, and suddenly I felt the best I had in days.

Li'l shifted around on her perch until she faced me again and waited until my laughter grew weak enough that I could hear her. "That's some laugh you have there,

Princess!" Li'l declared as I hiccuped my way to silence. "Did you get that when you became a frog or have you had it all along?"

"It's my laugh no matter who or what I am. My real name is Princess Emeralda, and his is Prince Eadric. I'm the only child of King Limelyn and Queen Chartreuse of the Kingdom of Greater Greensward. Eadric is the eldest son of the rulers of Upper Montevista." Proud of my royal heritage, I was sure that these creatures couldn't help but respect me now, so I was stunned by the reception my news received.

"Yeah, right," squeaked a voice.

"Then I'm King Mouseworthy!" squeaked another.

The creatures acted as if they'd heard the funniest thing in the world. Li'l Stinker laughed so hard that she tumbled off her rafter and flapped wildly, trying to regain her balance.

Indignant, I tried to shout over their laughter. "But I really am a princess! I can play the lute and embroider and sing and dance and do all the other things that princesses are supposed to do, although not as well as my mother would like. I can also do some other things that most princesses can't do. I can count and read and—"

"Did you say read?" asked Li'l, suddenly becoming serious.

"Why, yes," I said. "And I can swim, although I

couldn't do that before I became a frog. I can—"

"All right! I believe you! That's quite a list of accomplishments," said Li'l.

"It sure is!" chimed in a breathy voice. "I wish I could count. It would probably help me with some of my patterns."

My legs were beginning to itch. The rash was spreading. "Now it's your turn," I said, feeling moderately appeased. "I want to hear everyone else's names."

"That's easy enough," said the bat. "I'm Li'l, as you know, and in the cage below you are the spiders, Eenie, Meenie, and Moe. They used to live by the broom in the corner, but Vannabe found them and stuck them in a cage."

"We had another brother named Miney," whispered a tiny voice, "but the witch stepped on him when she caught us."

"I'm so sorry!" I said, furiously scratching behind my eardrum.

"It's one of the hazards of being a spider," said the voice sadly.

"Clifford and Louise live in the cage next to the spiders," continued Li'l. "Clifford and Louise are the mice who used to live under the bed. They've been together for a long time, so they tend to finish each other's sentences."

"Vannabe said she got tired—"

"—of hearing us scurry around."

"She put us in the cage—"

"—and we don't have anywhere to go."

"It's so boring!"

"We used to have the best adventures!"

"You wouldn't believe—"

"—what we found in the walls!"

"Some things are better left alone," said Li'l. "And that brings us to Fang. Fang has lived here since Vannabe moved in. She found him in the yard and put him in a cage her very first day. Fang doesn't talk much, so I'll tell you a bit about him. His cage is on the floor in the corner. It's the biggest cage in the cottage, but it's not nearly big enough for Fang. He was a large snake when he got here and he's grown since then."

A snake, I thought. Even if it was in a cage, the thought of a snake in the room made my heart beat faster and my skin feel cold and clammy.

"It's our turn!" breathed one of the spiders. "I want to hear how the two frogs were enchanted."

"Go ahead, princess!" squeaked a mouse.

"Tell us how—"

"—you became a frog!"

With a snake in the room, all I wanted to do was hide, but it seemed only fair that I answer. I swallowed hard and tried to speak normally. "Actually," I began, "it was Eadric who became a frog first. He said something to a witch that she didn't like and she turned him into a frog. Then when I kissed him so he would turn back into a prince, I turned into a frog, too. When we first saw Vannabe, we thought she was the witch who did it, but it wasn't her at all."

"Are you kidding?" said Li'l. "Vannabe couldn't turn a cabbage into coleslaw. She's trying to be a witch, but she doesn't have the knack for it."

"If she's not a witch, what does she want with Eadric and me? What is she going to do with those plants she found?"

"I'll tell you if you really want to know," said the bat.

"She'd be the one to tell," whispered one of the spiders in a voice so soft I might have imagined it. "Li'l Stinker has lived here most of her life. She's tied to that rafter with a piece of twine. It's too short to reach any of the cages, or one of us would have helped her untie it long ago. I've seen her try many a time, but that knot lasts like iron. I wish I could get up there to see what kind of knot the old witch used."

"Moe's very interested in knots. Eenie and I like to try different designs in our webs, but our brother has made knots his life study. You can see some of our handiwork on the broom against the back wall. Eenie, Miney, Moe, and I did it before the witch caught us."

"I'm sure you're very talented," I said.

"If you all are finished talking, I'll tell her about

87

Vannabe now. I refuse to try to speak over your cackling!" Li'l glared at each of the cages before swinging around to face me. "I'm going to have to give you a little history first. Vannabe has lived here for about a year. I'm the only one who's been here longer than that. I used to live here with the old witch, Mudine. She was a nice old lady, although kind of crazy toward the end. Hardly anybody came by because she didn't like company and she made people feel uncomfortable. She had me live with her only because she didn't like the bugs. The old woman thought cleaning was a waste of her time, so there were always plenty of bugs and I was here to eat them."

Li'l sighed and rearranged her wings. "Those were the good old days. That witch could do real magic and some days this place was hopping! But Mudine was old even when I first came to live with her, and her health wasn't good. Then she got sick and she couldn't take care of the animals anymore, so she let them all out of their cages. By then she was too weak to undo my twine, so I was still here when she lay down on her bed and disappeared in a puff of smoke.

"We'd known that a young woman from one of the farms had been snooping around for some time. We didn't let on, but we knew. The day the old witch vanished, Vannabe took the place over. The puff of smoke was still fogging up the room when that woman barged in and made herself at home. As far as I can tell, she hasn't even a hint of magic in her. Her only claim to fame is that she can read, which, I admit, is an accomplishment in itself. Why, these days the best witches are the ones with the talent who can also read. You have to read the old spells, you see. Passing them down by word of mouth can be a bit shaky. People forget things, mispronounce a word or two ... Who knows what can happen then?

"Anyway, Vannabe really wants to be a witch, but it takes more than just wanting. You have to have some talent or you can do only the simplest spells, the kind you just read from the book. Vannabe's not interested in the basic spells. She's got it in her head that to be a real witch she has to do big, showy magic, the kind that would impress lots of people. She doesn't realize that the little magic is powerful, too."

"But if she doesn't have the ability to do the magic, why is she here?"

"I can't answer that one. Maybe she doesn't realize she can't do it yet, maybe she's too stubborn to give up, or maybe her life on the farm was so bad, she'd rather be here."

"What is she looking for now?" I asked.

"She has some idea about trying one of Mudine's fancier spells," said Li'l. "The spell requires some unusual ingredients like that dragon's breath on the shelf next to you. See it there—it's the pretty bottle with the swirly colors. It was part of Mudine's collection. Vannabe would never have gotten it on her own."

"What is the spell for?"

"Nothing unusual. She thinks it will give her everlasting youth and beauty. These things usually backfire, but there's no telling her that."

"Tell the frog about the rest of the ingredients." The voice was dry and raspy. Just hearing it made my skin crawl. *The snake,* I thought, shuddering.

"Oh, yeah," said Li'l. "Aside from some rare plants, all she needed were the tongues and toes of talking frogs. She has plans for you and your friend. Your fate was sealed as soon as she heard you talk. That's why she wanted to keep you calm. She wouldn't want you to damage those precious tongues and toes right when she was about to use them."

"Our tongues and toes! She wouldn't listen when we tried to tell her that we aren't really frogs! I even told her that my parents would reward her, but it didn't make any difference."

"Of course not. If you were humans, you wouldn't be of any use to her. She needs talking frogs to make her spell work. No gold or jewels would get her what she wants. Only the right ingredients could do that, and that includes you, or at least parts of you."

"What are we going to do?"

"Hope that she doesn't find the plants she's looking for. She can't do the spell without them."

"You really do know everything that goes on around here," I said.

"I should. I've been here the longest and can see just about everything from my rafter," Li'l said proudly.

Wind blew through the cracks in the shutters, sending dust and scraps of litter swirling around the cottage. The room grew dark and rain pattered on the roof. It lasted only a few seconds, then abruptly stopped. The wind blew again and I coughed at the swirling dust. When the rain came in earnest, it was heavier and louder than before. A steady drizzle fell through a dozen holes in the roof, leaving damp spots on the table and floor. Li'l edged along her rafter, avoiding the worst of the leaks.

Everyone had grown quiet when the rain began, lulled by the steady drumming. Although the sound was soothing, I was unable to relax, for I'd begun to feel a prickling down my spine as if someone was watching me. Certain that I would have noticed Vannabe's return, I glanced over my shoulder. At first I thought that no one was there, but then I noticed the jar of eyeballs. Every one was focused on me. It made me feel the way I had on the rare occasion that my father had me sit beside him on the raised dais of the throne room while he received petitioners. Courtiers and commoners alike had stared at me as if hoping I'd make a fool of myself so they'd have something to talk about later. I'd hated the feeling then and I hated it even more now; these eyes were unsettling even when they weren't looking at me. I tried to ignore them, but it was nearly impossible.

In a way, it was almost a relief when the door squealed on its ancient hinges and Vannabe stalked into the room: all the eyes turned to watch her. Tossing her dripping sack on the table, she hurried to light the lantern. I crouched down and pretended to be asleep, but my heart began to race when the witch walked toward my shelf. *This is it*, I thought. If anyone had ever told me that I'd end up as a frog used in a witch's spell, I would have sworn he was crazy. But now ...! The witch stopped beside my cage and I held my breath. I was positive that I was about to lose some of my favorite body parts until I realized that Vannabe was looking through the pile of books and not at me.

"It's somewhere in one of these," Vannabe muttered to herself. "The old woman kept good records. I'm sure she wrote about the plants I need." She took the dragon's skull from the pile of books and set it aside, then selected some books and carried them to the table. A few minutes later she was back, shuffling through the books again.

Each time the witch approached our cage, I pretended to be asleep. I opened my eyes only when I was sure she was looking the other way, and then I opened them only a little. I was glad of this the next time she passed by, for she paused by our cage to look at us. Even with my eyes closed, I could feel the woman's eyes boring into me.

"The frogs' tongues and toes can wait until I'm about to start," Vannabe decided after a long silence. "They'll be more potent if they're nice and fresh."

I heard her move on to the books and look them over one more time. A chill crept through me and I fought to keep it from showing. Vannabe selected a book and returned to the table. The room grew quiet, and although I knew she was lost in her studies, I was too scared to open my eyes.

Tongues and toes, I thought. *She's going to take our tongues and toes. Even if she doesn't kill us, we'll be maimed for the rest of our lives. What are we going to do?*

It was late by the time Vannabe found the book that she needed. Musty and yellowing with age, it contained notes written years before by the old witch. Vannabe pored over the pictures, looking for the plants named in the spell. "Found it!" she said at last. "But according to this I need the stems, not the leaves. Good," she said, yawning. "I'll get them first thing in the morning. Tomorrow is the big day!" Still studying the drawing, the witch fell asleep with the book clutched in her hands.

When I was sure that Vannabe was asleep, I hurried

to Eadric's side and shook him as hard as I could. "Eadric!" I whispered in his eardrum. "We have to think of something. We have to get out of here tonight. She's going to cut out your tongue tomorrow! She's going to cut off your toes! Please, Eadric! You have to wake up!"

Eadric groaned and raised his head to look at me through heavily lidded eyes. "Leave me alone, Emma," he said. "I'm too tired to talk."

"You're awake, Eadric! You're awake!" Eadric's head sank down onto his arm. I grabbed his shoulders in desperation and shook him. "We have to talk now, Eadric! We only have until tomorrow morning!"

Eadric began to snore. I sank to the floor of the cage in despair. *What am I going to do?* I thought for the hundredth time that day. Fat tears rolled down my cheeks and plopped onto the bottom of the cage.

"Hey, it's not that bad," Li'l said from her rafter. "If he woke up enough to talk, you'll probably be able to wake him completely in the morning. Leave him alone and get some rest yourself. You're going to need it tomorrow."

"I can't sleep, Li'l—I'm too scared," I protested. "And even if I could, this itchy rash is driving me crazy."

"A rash, huh? I can't keep you from being afraid, but I may know of a remedy for that rash. We'll need light for it, though, so we'll see about it tomorrow. Now relax and try to sleep. Nothing is hopeless, at least not yet."

Ten

"Psst!" The sound woke me from a restless sleep. "Psst! Emma, wake up!"

Still groggy, I lifted my head. At first I felt disoriented, the cage and the drafty room unfamiliar and threatening. Then I remembered where I was and what was supposed to happen and suddenly I was wide awake.

"Emma! Wake up! Vannabe's gone! Hurry—I thought of something!"

"I'm awake." I blinked and looked up.

"Finally!" said the bat, and she dropped like a stone from her perch to the stack of books on the shelf.

"Li'l!" I exclaimed. "What are you doing?"

"I have an idea," she panted. "I was thinking about your rash and I remembered this book." Stretching her tether as far as it would go, the bat tugged one of the books off the pile and dropped it onto the shelf. "There!" she said triumphantly. "I think that's the right one."

"What are you talking about?" I asked. "How is a book going to help anything?"

"Open it up and take a look. If I remember right, there should be a great spell for getting rid of rashes."

"The rash isn't my biggest worry now, Li'l."

"I know, but the book with the spell for rashes has a lot of other useful spells, too. I can't read, so I'm not sure if this is the right book. Go ahead, take a look."

"But I can't, Li'l! I can't do magic! I make a mess of it every time!"

"What are you talking about? All you have to do is read it! You can do that, can't you?"

"Yes, of course, but you don't know me! I can botch even the simplest spells! You should have seen what happened when I tried to clean my chamber using magic! My bed still makes itself whether I'm in it or not!"

"It's up to you. If you'd rather lose your tongue than try …"

"All right! I get your point! I guess it wouldn't hurt to try." I reached for the cover of the book, but my arms weren't long enough to touch it. Even turning sideways and shoving my leg between the bars of the cage wasn't enough.

"I can't reach it!" I said, stretching my leg as far as I could. Hoping to find something that I could use to extend my reach, I looked about my cage. There was nothing close enough to the cage that might be useful, and the only thing inside the cage was Eadric, lying on his back with his belly in the air and his limbs flopping at his sides in a most unfroglike position. His legs were long, longer than mine, and if I could wake him …

At first I was gentle, shaking his shoulder, whispering his name and poking him in the ribs, but when that didn't work, I tried more enthusiastic means. Shouting his name just made him twitch in his sleep. Pulling his leg made him roll over. Finally, I tried lightly slapping his cheeks.

"It wasn't me, Mother," Eadric mumbled, brushing away my hand. "I would never put a mouse in Nanny's ale, even if she did leave the room to use the privy."

I glanced up at the bat, who had returned to her rafter and was hanging upside down, watching me. "Li'l, you said he would probably wake up today, but look at him. What am I going to do?"

"I suppose you could try the remedy used on those nitwits Snow White and Sleeping Beauty. I told you they were given the same potion, remember?"

"Right, right, I remember now. They were both princesses and they were both woken by princes, if I remember correctly. And the princes both … aw, Li'l, I'm not going to have to kiss him, am I?"

"Only if you want him to wake up."

"But I told you what happened last time."

"I'd be real surprised if you turned into anything else now. But whatever you're going to do, you'd better hurry. You don't have much time here. Vannabe won't be gone forever."

"I know, but … oh, all right. I guess even if we did turn into something else, it couldn't be worse than being a frog." I squatted beside him and placed my hands on either side of his face. "It's funny," I said. "He's finally getting his kiss and all he had to do for it was oversleep." I was about to kiss him when something else occurred to me. "Li'l?" I tilted my head to look up at the bat. "If I kiss him and he does wake up, I'm not going to have to marry him, am I? I mean, both of those princes married the girls they woke this way."

"Naw, you won't have to marry him unless you want to."

"Good! I want to keep my options open." I kept my eyes open as well this time, thinking half seriously that that might keep me from turning into something else. His lips were cool and smooth, just like the first time, and I had barely taken my lips from his when his eyelids fluttered open and he gazed up into my eyes.

"Well, hello there, beautiful! Is there something you want to tell me?" Eadric said, leering froggishly.

"What do you mean? I was just—"

"Don't get me wrong! I like being kissed by beautiful young ladies; I just wasn't expecting it, that's all."

"I wasn't kissing you. I mean, I was, but it was only to wake you up!"

"And I liked it! You can wake me that way every morning, and put me to sleep that way, too." Eadric winked and reached for my shoulders.

Pushing his hands away, I hopped to the other side of the cage, giving me space and the time I needed to explain. "I was kissing you only because you've been asleep since the day before yesterday! I warned you about that worm! But no, you had to eat a worm doused in sleeping potion! You had to sleep when you should have been trying to help me find a way to escape! I've been scared to death while you've been dreaming the time away and it just wasn't fair!"

"Emma," Eadric began.

"Never mind. We don't have time to talk now. The witch is going to be back soon to chop off our toes and cut out our tongues. Now get up and come help me! We have to look through this book and I can't reach it. Do you think you can turn the pages?"

Eadric looked thoroughly confused, but he didn't question me. With a long-suffering sigh, he struggled to his feet and hopped to the side of the cage. Crouching down, he stuck his arm between the bars, but it wasn't quite long enough.

"Maybe your leg," I said.

I was overjoyed when his longer legs reached easily.

"What is it we're looking for?" he asked.

"Just turn the pages when I tell you to," I said. "I'll let you know when I find it."

"See if you can find the rash spell first," said Li'l. "Then we'll know if it's the right book."

Eadric turned around with a jerk, aware of Li'l for the first time. Trying to look nonchalant, he leaned over until his lips brushed my eardrum. "Who's the bat?" he whispered.

"She's a friend," I explained. "Her name is Li'l. Now be quiet and let me read this!"

I studied the book of spells, concentrating on some while skipping over others. At my direction, Eadric slowly turned one page after another until I saw what I wanted near the back of the book.

"Here it is!" I said, pointing to a spell. "Rash Rid—rid yourself of that itchy rash in those hard-to-reach places."

Li'l shifted nervously on her seat atop the stack of books. "Try it. It'll be good practice."

"Do I just read this out loud, Li'l?"

"Read it with feeling, Emma! And make big, dramatic gestures with your arms!"

"Anything special?"

"No, no! Just be dramatic!"

"All right, here goes!" I read the spell with as much emotion as I could, waving my arms and gesturing wildly.

Red blotches, rosy bumps,
Itchy spots, scaly lumps,
All you rashes here and there
Under shirts and underwear
On the legs and on the feet,
Don't look now, you're in retreat!
Begone, rash, and nevermore
Irritate my tender pore!

Despite the closed windows and doors, a blast of cold air blew through the cottage. For the briefest instant, I felt prickly all over. I looked down at my leg. It was the same smooth green it had been before I got the rash. I twisted around to look at my back. It, too, was smooth and green. All the itchy bumps had disappeared.

"Good job," said Li'l. "You know, that works for pimples and boils, too. If you were a human, you'd never have another blemish for the rest of your life!"

"That was amazing! If these spells really work, this book is incredible! Look at some of these other spells, Eadric. Here's one for skin softening. It says it will make your skin as soft as a baby's bottom. You can have the hair color you've always wanted with Hair So Nu. This one's called Body Beautiful. It says you can eat what you want without gaining a pound. I wonder if there's a spell that would make me graceful."

"They look like a lot of useless beauty tips to me,"

said Eadric. "How would any of these help us with this witch?"

"They're not all useless. Look, this could be a big help. Squeak Be Gone—squeaky hinges squeak no more. How about Grow Rite—grow the biggest vegetables in the marketplace! Easy Open—open any container without breaking a nail. Listen, they're so simple." Using my normal reading voice, I said,

> Unlatch, unlock, undo, untie,
> In the twinkling of an eye.
> Open ye lock,
> Lift ye latch,
> Remove ye block,
> Release ye catch.

A sound like thunder shook the cottage. A tiny whirlwind twirled debris around and around the room. Then, with a pop, every container in the cottage opened. Lids flew off boxes, corks flew out of bottles, shutters swung open, the door to the cottage slammed back with a crash, the bat's tether twitched loose, and every cage opened with a *whoosh!*

"Would you look at that!" exclaimed Li'l.

"Li'l, you're a genius. You were right about this book!"

"Ladies, the door is open! Don't just stand there

talking!" said Eadric. "Let's get out of here before the witch gets back! Look, there go some mice."

Clifford and Louise had wasted no time and were already crossing the threshold. "Watch out, Emma!" called Clifford.

"Fang is loose!" shouted Louise.

"I'd forgotten all about the snake!" I gasped. "Where do you suppose he is?"

"Snake? What snake?" said Eadric.

"There was a big snake in one of the cages. His name is Fang," I explained.

"Of course it is," muttered Eadric. "What else would it be?"

"He's probably long gone by now," said Li'l. "He never was very sociable, so I doubt he hung around. I have to tell you, though, Emma, I'm proud of you! I knew you could do it as soon as you said you could read."

"So why didn't you have me read that spell right away? What if I hadn't read it at all?"

"I wasn't sure which spells were in that book. I just knew that they were simple spells and that a couple might have worked one way or another. I've never read them myself. You're the first creature I've met who could read."

"What about the spiders?" I asked, remembering the smallest of Vannabe's captives. "Are they still in their cage?"

"They were the first ones out," said Li'l. "I saw them going down a crack in the floorboards."

"What's that?" squeaked Eadric, pointing toward the fireplace, his eyes bulging even more than usual. Convinced that he was overreacting, I looked to where he was pointing. I must admit that if frogs could break out in a cold sweat, I would have done it then. Something still slopped around inside the barrel labeled *Trash Can,* but it didn't look any different than it had before. However, the lid had popped off the barrel labeled *Trash Can't,* leaving it open to the air. Three slimy tentacles writhed over the rim, probing the side of the barrel. I shrieked when another rose up and slapped the wall with a soggy squelch.

"Dang," said Li'l, fluttering her wings in agitation. "Looks like Vannabe's got herself two Trash Cans!"

I gulped and whispered hoarsely, "You mean one barrel was called a Trash Can't …"

"Because the trash couldn't get out of it. But it sure can now!"

"Which makes it a Trash Can!"

"Yup!" said Li'l.

"Another reason we should get out of here as fast as we can. Look at those things!" Eadric's lips crinkled in disgust when an unattached tentacle slid to the floor and oozed toward the table, leaving a slime trail behind it. "Let's go somewhere safe!"

"He's got a point," I said. "See you later, Li'l."

"Emma, before you go," called the bat, "take this with you." Li'l flapped down to the shelf beside Eadric and me. Wrapping a wing around the vial of dragon's breath, she dragged it to us. "Without this, she won't have any reason to look for other talking frogs."

"But won't she come after us if she thinks we took it?"

"She won't know we took it if she doesn't see us with it, now, will she? And she won't see us with it if we're gone when she gets back." Eadric grabbed the vial with both hands and dragged it to the edge of the shelf.

I waved good-bye to Li'l and followed Eadric. Together, we jumped to the floor, then quickly hopped to the threshold.

"Wait," I told Eadric. I turned back into the room and looked up at the shelf. The bat still stood where we had left her. Her head and wings drooped and she looked so forlorn that I felt like crying.

"Li'l, aren't you coming?" I asked.

"No," said Li'l. "I think I'm going to stay here. I've spent most of my life in this cottage and I don't have anywhere else to go."

"You could come with us," I suggested.

The bat's expression brightened momentarily; then she shook her head and frowned. "It's no good," she said. "I'm meant to be a witch's bat. It's what I've always been and it's what I'll always be."

"But she'll tie you up again!"

"Not in this cottage. Not after that spell. Nothing is going to stay closed or tied in here unless she finds another spell to reverse it. Now hurry and get out of here. I can hear her coming."

I hopped to the doorway and looked out. Although I could see all the way to the other side of the clearing, there was no sign of the witch. "I don't see her. How can you hear her all the way over here?"

"You're questioning a bat's hearing?" asked Eadric. "If the bat says the witch is coming, the witch is coming. Let's go. This thing is heavy."

But I still couldn't leave. "Li'l!" I called. "Vannabe isn't even a real witch. If you want to be a witch's bat, you can come live with my aunt. She's the Green Witch and she's much nicer than Vannabe. Come with us and I'll take you to meet her. I know you'd get along wonderfully!"

"I don't know, Emma. Are you sure about your aunt? Maybe she already has a bat."

"No, no bats, only a small green snake who's free to come and go as she pleases."

"Li'l, please come," said Eadric. "She's not going to move unless you do."

"All right, I'm coming!" said Li'l. "But you go on ahead. I have to get something."

"You heard her," said Eadric. "Let's go!"

With his arms still wrapped around the vial of dragon's breath, Eadric hopped out the door and into the clearing beyond. I hopped along at his side, turning around every so often to look for Li'l. We didn't stop to catch our breath until we reached the tall grass. "Do you see her yet?" I asked. "Do you see Li'l anywhere?"

"No, there's no sign of the bat, but look there! The witch is back!"

"Eadric, Li'l hasn't come out yet! If the witch catches her ..."

Vannabe saw the open door the moment she entered the clearing. With a shout of rage, she hiked up her skirts and ran toward the cottage. Even though we knew she couldn't see us, Eadric and I crouched in the tall grass, our hearts pounding in terror.

We saw Vannabe drop her sack on the ground and dart into the cottage. A scream rang through the clearing. Moments later Li'l shot out of the cottage at full speed with the witch close behind. Waving her broom wildly, Vannabe cursed and tried to knock the bat to the ground. When Li'l pumped her wings and flew higher, Vannabe gave up and hurled her broom away in disgust.

"Then get out of here, stupid bat! I don't need you anyway!" she shrieked, her face twisted in anger. Clenching her fists, Vannabe glared at the peaceful clearing as if it might give her the answers. "Who did this?

Who freed my creatures and ruined my spell?"

"I guess she hasn't noticed that the dragon's breath is gone yet," I whispered.

Vannabe ran back into her cottage. A bloodcurdling scream rattled the window frames.

"I think she just noticed," said Eadric.

Movement in the cloudless sky made me look up. It was Li'l, zigzagging above the clearing as she searched for us.

"Li'l, over here!" I called softly.

Turning abruptly, the bat headed straight for Eadric and me.

"As soon as she gets here, do you mind if we get going?" asked Eadric. "I feel a little conspicuous lugging this thing around."

"Sorry," I said. "We can go now."

Li'l swooped overhead and fled into the forest. We tried to follow as quickly as we could, but the vial of dragon's breath slowed our progress. It was an awkward object to carry and made hopping difficult.

"Tell me again why I'm hauling this stuff around," Eadric said. "If we're just taking it so the witch can't use it, why can't I put it down now and leave it here?"

"Think of it this way," I said. "This is the only container in the whole cottage that didn't open. It must be pretty strong stuff. We don't want just anybody to find it.

And you never know, maybe we can use it ourselves someday."

"Now you sound like my mother. I don't think she's ever thrown anything away in her whole life. If we start keeping everything we might use someday, we're going to have to build a wagon to haul it around. All I can say is, this dragon's breath had better be worth it. And what's this about taking Li'l to see your aunt Grassina?"

"We have to go there anyway," I said. "I'm not going to fool around anymore. This time I'm going straight to her tower at the castle. If she still isn't there, why, we'll find someplace safe to wait until she comes back. We know that the witch who cast the spell is dead, so Grassina is the only one we can ask. If anyone can help us, it'll be my aunt."

"I don't think you realize how dangerous a trip to the castle would be. It's a long way from here and even if you did reach it, the guards wouldn't allow you within the castle walls. Then, if you could somehow make it inside, the dogs would get you or the servants would squash you on sight. Are you sure you want to do this?"

"I wish you'd have more faith in me. I got us out of that cage, didn't I?"

"Not because you'd planned it that way!"

"It doesn't matter," I said. "It won't be any more dangerous for me to go to the castle than it would be to stay here."

"For us, you mean," said Eadric.

I shook my head. "You don't have to go with me. You said you didn't want to talk to my aunt. She's a 'spell-casting witch,' remember?"

Eadric sighed. "If you're going, then I'm going, too. I think this is a foolish idea, but I can't let you go on your own. I'll do what I can to protect you. Don't forget, I have an interest in your welfare. If Grassina is your aunt, she can't be all bad, and if she turns you back into a human, I want to be there."

"So she can turn you back into a prince as well?"

Eadric gave me a lopsided grin. "If she can. Besides, maybe I'll get lucky and you'll give me another kiss."

Eleven

$\mathcal{B}$ecause we had arrived at the witch's cottage shut inside a musty sack, I'd had no idea that Vannabe had carried us from the swamp into the forest until I saw the towering trees that ringed the clearing. As Eadric and I passed the first weathered trunks, I realized that I hadn't the faintest clue which way we should go. Tall trees blocked the sunlight, leaving the forest floor dark and gloomy. We passed beneath an old oak, hopping over its gnarled roots and the carpet of decaying leaves from years past.

"This place is spooky," I said, glancing over my shoulder.

"I like the dark," said a voice, and we looked up to see Li'l hanging from a branch, huddled against the trunk of the tree. "It makes me feel safer. I think I was born somewhere around here, although I don't remember it very well."

"I have no idea how to reach the castle from here," I

said. "Do you think you could fly above the trees and see if you can find it? That would help ever so much."

"If you really want me to, I suppose I could go look. But it's awfully bright up there …"

"If you don't mind. It's the only castle around with green pennants flying from the turrets. You can't miss it."

Li'l nodded. "I'll be right back."

We watched her flap her wings and fly between the branches in fits and starts.

"Does she seem nervous to you?" Eadric asked.

"Very," I said, "but you can't blame her. This is the first time she's been outside since she was a baby. I think it would be frightening for her. So much of it will be new."

"And her flying …"

"Give her some time. Don't forget that she's been tethered to a rafter most of her life. I doubt she's been able to do much flying."

"I have to set this down," Eadric said, placing the vial on the ground and rolling his shoulders to work out the kinks in his muscles. "That vial is heavier than it looks. Of course, if you kissed me again, I might have enough energy to haul it around some more."

I sighed and shook my head. "I don't understand. Why do you keep asking for a kiss?"

Eadric shrugged. "Habit, I guess."

"Well, I guess I'm in the habit of saying no!"

"Rejected again," he said, quirking up one corner of his mouth in a half smile. "I must admit, I'm getting used to it."

Leaves rustled as a squirrel darted along the branch of a tree. We both glanced up, and I, at least, felt very small, dwarfed by the immensity of the forest. The trees where we stood were ancient, their trunks so thick that I couldn't have put my arms around them even when I was a human. Broken branches littered the ground, and here and there we could see where one of the mature trees had fallen, exposing a patch of the forest floor to the sun. Young saplings were quick to grow in such spots, greedily seeking their share of the sunlight. With our backs to the meadow, the forest seemed to go on forever. It would be easy to get lost in such a place.

"You know," said Eadric, "it might be a real help to have your bat friend with us. If she can scout ahead, she should be able to keep us going in the right direction."

"Even if she weren't able to help us, I couldn't have left her behind. No one deserved to be left in that awful place."

"I am glad you think so," breathed a voice that sent a chill up my spine. I turned my head toward the sound. Dead leaves whispered beneath the biggest snake that I had ever seen. Four black stripes ran down his gray and white body. A streak of black accented each eye. I froze, unable to move as the snake stared into my eyes. "What is wrong?" breathed the snake. "Do you not recognize me?"

"Are you ... Fang?" I asked through a throat tight with fear.

"At your service," the snake hissed, coiling his length under him. "You mentioned your destination. I believe that you could use my company."

"Why would we want you along?" Eadric asked, his voice quavering.

The snake swung his head around to face my friend, looking him up and down as if appraising his next meal. "Because I know what lives in this forest. Witches have lived here for centuries, and the spillover from their magic has changed even the trees themselves. But you need not fear the magical beings, for they will see you as an animal and therefore one who belongs. Still, you would not make it through without me, for your indiscretions will soon attract the attention of predators. Without my protection, your journey is doomed before you begin."

Great! I thought. *Even the snake is a critic!* I swallowed past the lump in my throat and tried my best to look brave. "So you're not going to eat us?"

"I do not eat creatures who have helped me. You freed me from a cage so small I feared I would soon go insane. I owe you far more than I can repay by a simple trip through the forest. No, I swear upon my honor as a snake that I shall not eat you." Fang dipped his head to me in a gesture both elegant and noble.

It was up to me to set an example. I resolved not to let anyone see either my fear or the revulsion I felt at being around a snake.

"Does that include my companions, too?"

"Of course. I will—"

"Snake! Snake!" shrieked Li'l, flitting back and forth just above our heads. "Look out, frogs! That's Fang and he's going to get you! What can I do? What can I do?"

The poor bat was frantic and I began to worry that she might injure herself in her frenzy. Apparently, I wasn't the only one concerned, but the snake was more disapproving of the commotion than he was worried about her well-being.

"Would you be so kind as to do something about Li'l?" Fang said in a voice that made my skin crawl. "She's drawing too much attention to us. If you don't stop her immediately, I shall."

I couldn't watch my friend risk her life, but trusting a snake went against all my instincts. Setting aside my misgivings, I waved my arms frantically above my head and shouted as loudly as I could. "Li'l! No! He's a friend!" I hoped it was the truth.

Li'l veered away in midflight and landed on the ground behind Eadric. "Has Emma lost her mind?" she whispered. "How could any snake be her friend?"

"Fang said he owes her a debt, so he's going with us. He promises not to eat us."

"Are you sure he can be trusted? He was always very polite, but he never seemed to want to be anyone's friend. How do we know this isn't a trick? From what I've heard, snakes are pretty sneaky characters."

"What do you suggest we do about it?" whispered Eadric. "He's bigger than the rest of us put together. I don't think it would do any good to tell him not to come."

"Maybe," said Li'l, "but we can keep an eye on him. We'll take turns watching him tonight. I'll take first watch."

"You won't need to wake me when it's my turn," said Eadric. "I won't be able to sleep with him around anyway."

"What are you two talking about?" I asked, although I'd already heard their conversation and feared that Fang had as well. I hopped closer to my friends while Fang raised his head and stared at them through slitted eyes.

"Nothing," said Li'l in a tiny voice as she noticed Fang watching her. She crouched down to hide behind Eadric until all I could see were the tips of her wings. "I was about to show Eadric my twine. It's my only possession and I couldn't leave it behind."

"You risked your life for a piece of twine?" I

116

exclaimed.

Li'l peeked out from behind Eadric. "That wasn't the only reason I stayed. I moved the book so Vannabe wouldn't know what we'd done. Anyway, the string will be really useful. We can tie the dragon's breath to someone's back with it. Here," she said, handing it to Eadric.

Eadric examined the coarse brown string, turning it over in his hands. "Fine. Tie it to my back. At least that way my arms won't get tired anymore."

"If you have finished your conversation, may I suggest that we move on?" hissed Fang. "You are wasting daylight hours."

At the sound of Fang's voice, Li'l ducked down behind Eadric again. "I saw the castle. I can show you how to get there," she whispered.

"That would be a big help," I said, trying to be encouraging.

"Uh, Fang," said Eadric, "I'd feel a lot more comfortable if you went in front of Emma and me."

"Excellent thinking," said the snake. "I'll scout ahead for trouble." Li'l took off, and the snake watched to see where she headed before slithering off into the leaf litter.

It was up to me to tie the vial to Eadric's back. Although frogs can do many things with their fingers, tying knots is not one of them. "You'd think four fingers would be enough to tie a knot," I said, fumbling with the

117

twine. "But these things just don't work the same as human fingers do. I wish Moe were here. He was the one who knew all about knots."

"Who is Moe?" Eadric asked. "Not another friend of yours? You collect friends like black tunics collect dandruff."

I sighed. I'd forgotten that Eadric had slept through an entire day. "Never mind," I told him. "Someday I'll tell you all about everything you missed while you were asleep. But right now, you can tell me something. What are you and Li'l up to?"

"Li'l and I don't trust that snake and we want to keep an eye on him. I wouldn't want him behind us anyway. Who knows when he might get tired of watching such tempting morsels hopping along right under his nose? A promise is easy to forget when you're hungry."

"He was hungry when he left the cottage. If he wanted to eat us, wouldn't he have done it already?"

"My dear Princess Emeralda, you are awfully naïve, or perhaps I should say that you're too trusting. You think that everyone is going to be your friend until you learn otherwise."

"Look who's talking! You're the one who ate the witch's worm! But you're wrong, you know. I didn't trust you at first."

"Then you trust everyone but me."

"That's not true. I trust you now."

"Good! But you still shouldn't trust that snake. I don't think we need him, despite what he says."

"You don't think we're in danger in these woods?"

"I think the biggest danger we'll face just invited itself along."

"I don't know—these woods are awfully creepy. I can't wait to get through them and back into the sunlight." I looked up at the leafy canopy.

Li'l flew off periodically to check our progress, then returned to keep us headed in the right direction. However, we saw little of Fang for the rest of the day. He scouted ahead as he'd said he would, and if he came across anything dangerous, he didn't tell us about it.

We saw some strange sights as we traveled, things that could be attributed only to magic. Trees seemed to move in most untreelike ways, bending with a fluid grace to lean toward neighbors, the rustle of their leaves almost sounding like words. I swore I saw one pull up its roots and move into a patch of sunlight, but when we reached the spot the roots looked as if they'd been growing there for years.

We'd been traveling through the woods for a few hours when the ground began to shake and we heard the thudding footsteps of a large, heavy creature. Although the noise grew increasingly loud, distance and dense foliage kept the thing hidden from sight. Suddenly, there was a tremendous crash, followed by the shriek of splitting wood. The trees around us shuddered in sympathy, raining leaves like emerald teardrops. I jumped to avoid a falling twig, but the ground wasn't where I thought it would be and I landed in a depression nearly twice my height.

"Emma! What happened? Are you all right?" Eadric's shout made me cringe, for he had been loud and I knew the sound would carry.

"Shh!" I whispered. "Not so loud! I'm down here!"

Eadric's face appeared over the edge of the hole, peering down at me with a look of such concern that I immediately regretted scolding him. "Let me help you up," he said, extending his hand to take mine.

"You don't need to do that," I said, backing up a few steps. "I think I can make it. Watch out!" I tensed my legs and was about to leap when the ground shook with such force that the sides of the hole began to crumble, dropping clods of dirt onto my head and shoulders. A faint whimper came from above, and Eadric plopped into the hole beside me. The moment he landed, he shoved me back against the side of the depression and held me there, all the while looking as though he would like to disappear straight into the soil. There was a deafening thud, and something blew hot air reeking of brimstone into our hole.

"Frogs," grated a voice, sounding so disappointed that I almost spoke up. Eadric must have sensed this, for

120

he clapped his hand over my mouth until the creature took off with a great flapping of leathery wings that sent leaves and other debris swirling down around us.

"What was that?" I whispered once the sound had grown too faint to hear.

"A dragon!" Eadric breathed. "I didn't know there were any around here! Why, if I had my sword ..."

"You wouldn't be able to lift it! You're a frog, remember?"

"Oh, yeah. But as soon as I'm human again ..."

"Uh-huh," I said, finding it hard to believe that Eadric would ever face a dragon in any form whether he had a sword or not. "Come on. We have to get out of here if we're going to get changed back."

Jumping out of the hole was easy, but we'd gotten turned around and it took us a few minutes to find our original heading. The trees seemed to have moved as well, but we finally found our footprints and determined which direction we'd been going before. We also figured out what had made the hole: it looked like a giant footprint.

"Giants and dragons!" Eadric said, grinning from eardrum to eardrum. "I really will have to come back here with my sword!"

"Right," I said. "Whatever you say."

I began to notice other prints after that, like the enormous marks of a griffin's talon and paw. We saw additional signs of the dragon as well, for some of the trees were singed, and the bark had been rubbed off others. Sensitive to the forest now, I saw shadows where there was sound but no substance, flickering lights where there should have been none, but nothing else came to bother us. If we had passed through this forest in the witch's bag, it was just as well that we had done it in ignorance.

We had both been complaining of thirst for some time when we finally came across a pool of water. Although sheltered by the canopy of ancient interlocking branches, the water sparkled invitingly as if lying in the direct rays of the brightly shining sun.

"What are you waiting for?" Eadric asked when I hesitated. "It looks clean enough."

"Maybe so, but what do we really know about it? It could be enchanted or even poisoned. I'm not sure—"

I gasped, for the face and dripping locks of a beautiful, ageless nymph had broken the surface of the water. She looked around eagerly, but when she failed to see whatever it was that she was looking for, her perfect mouth twisted in a sulky pout and her aqua-colored eyes clouded over. Sighing loudly, the nymph rose gracefully from the water and stepped onto the bank. Although her long green hair reached past her knees, it did little to cover her naked form. Ignoring us, she dropped down on one of the larger flat rocks and began to comb her hair, her gaze as unfocused as a daydream.

Eadric sighed and I glanced in his direction. To my disgust, he was gazing longingly at the nymph like some lovesick squire who'd just discovered his true love.

"Eadric!" I said, jabbing him with my elbow. "What's wrong with you? She's a nymph! You know she has only one thing on her mind."

"I know," he said, his eyes glazing over. "And I'm a handsome prince...."

"Eadric, you're—" But my warning was too late, for Eadric had hopped onto the rock.

"You are the essence of beauty," he began, his eyes raised adoringly to the nymph's face. "You are my sun, my moon, my stars."

"You're a frog," she said, noticing him at last. "I don't talk to frogs."

"I'm not just a frog."

"You look like a frog to me," she said, the tiniest frown wrinkling her flawless brow.

"Yes, yes, of course I do, my sweet, but I'm really an enchanted prince!"

The nymph's eyes flickered with interest. "Prove it! Show me your crown or your jeweled sword!"

"I'm sorry, I don't have them with me."

"Oh," she said, her pout returning. "Then you'll have to leave. Someone important might come by at any moment."

"But I'm important! I'm—"

"You're a frog. Now go away. This is my pool and I don't allow frogs here. You lay those disgusting, gooey eggs and foul my nice clean water."

"But I'm a prince! I don't lay eggs! I won't—"

Tossing her hair over her shoulder with a dainty flip of her wrist, the nymph turned her back and pointedly ignored Eadric. He looked so crestfallen, I almost felt sorry for him. Almost, but not quite.

"But I *am* a prince!" he said when he joined me back on the bank.

"Not right now you're not, and it's a good thing, too! Nymphs drown princes, so be happy that she's not interested in you. It's the only reason you're still alive. The potion Vannabe put on that worm must have softened your brain. We'd better go before you make an even bigger fool of yourself."

I couldn't tell whether Eadric was upset by the nymph's rejection or because I'd called him a fool, but either way, he was in a sulky mood. It was probably just as well that he didn't feel like talking to me, since I was so irritated that I couldn't have said a pleasant word to him even if he'd paid me with all the mosquitoes in the forest.

Fuming silently at Eadric's foolishness, I was relieved to see a friendly face when Li'l found us on the forest floor. She'd come to tell us that we didn't have far to travel, but it was already getting too dark to see, though she seemed not to mind.

"I think we'd better stop now," I said, raising my hand and wiggling my fingers. "I can barely see my hand in front of my face."

"If you really want to," Li'l replied. "Although I think it's just getting nice out! But if you want to go to sleep, you should find a good place to hide. Who knows what comes out at night in these woods."

"I can think of one thing," Eadric said, spotting a sudden flash of light. "Fireflies! Ladies and gentlemen, I think dinner has arrived."

A firefly darted erratically through the gloom beneath the trees, its tiny light pinpointing its path. Despite the empty ache in my stomach, I was reluctant to try to catch one. I'd heard that fairies often flew about at night dressed in little more than twinkling lights. Because they were nasty when insulted, I shuddered to think what they might do if you tried to eat them. Eadric, however, had no such qualms and quickly set about catching his dinner. I laughed when I saw his throat lit up from inside. My guffaw was loud in the darkened night and sounded strange even in my own eardrums. I stopped abruptly. Frightened by the thought of the predators that might hear me, I no longer felt like laughing.

Eventually satisfied that they really were fireflies and not deceitful fairies, I flicked out my tongue, coiling it back with a tingle of anticipation. It wasn't bad.

While Eadric and I waited for another firefly to pass by, Li'l flew over to sit beside me. "How do they taste?" she asked.

"Delicious! And just think, a week ago you couldn't have paid me to eat a firefly!"

"A week ago I didn't know what they were," said Li'l. "I've never had one."

"Never?" I said. "Then you need to try them!"

Something rustled the leaves in the tree above us, prompting Li'l to look about nervously. Wrapping her wings around her body to make herself as small as she could, she shuffled toward me until we stood shoulder to wing.

Although the night sounds made me nervous as well, I was reluctant to let Li'l see it, as I was sure it would only add to her fear. "While you're here," I said, hoping to distract her, "there's something I've wanted to ask you. Back in the cottage, why did the 'open box' spell work even though I didn't gesture or use a dramatic voice like you told me to?"

Li'l shrugged her wings. "You don't have to do those things to make the spell work. I just like it better when it's done that way."

"You mean all that arm waving I did was just for show?"

"Yup."

"I thought it might be something special that Mudine did to make the spells more powerful."

"Nope."

"And what about the first spell? The one for rashes? It worked only on me, but when I did the spell to open boxes, it opened everything in the cottage."

"Actually, they both would have worked on everyone near you, but you were the only one with a rash. If you want a spell to be specific to one subject, you need to use something to focus it. You can point just about anything at your subject to aim the power."

"Like a magic wand?"

"Yup, although it doesn't have to be a wand. In fact, if a witch has had enough practice, pointing her finger works just fine."

I'd been watching Eadric while Li'l and I talked, amazed at how many insects he'd eaten. Neither our conversation nor the strangeness of the forest could distract him from the pursuit of food. "Will you look at that!" I said to Li'l. "If we don't stop talking and go catch some fireflies, Eadric'll eat them all himself!"

Li'l smiled halfheartedly and took to the air to chase her first firefly. Darting between the trees, she snatched insects from the air as if magnetically drawn to them. A day of flying had improved her rusty skills and she no longer seemed so hesitant.

We ate until we were full. Then Eadric and I made

ourselves cozy beds in the decomposing leaves while Li'l flew into the branches of the ancient maple above us. It didn't take Eadric long to fall asleep, but I lay awake far into the night. My thoughts bounced from one subject to another, and I found myself worrying about everything. What would happen to Eadric and me? Would Li'l like living with Grassina? How would I explain everything to my mother? Would the trees still be in the same place when we woke up in the morning? I wanted to go to sleep, but it seemed as if I'd forgotten how. Forcing myself to relax, I listened to the night sounds of the forest: Eadric snoring gently under his blanket of leaves; Li'l moving from one branch to another; a distant owl hooting softly; mice rustling the leaves in search of food; the creak of branches and the whispering of leaves. Eventually, the sounds grew fainter.

The next thing I knew I was in the Great Hall of my parents' castle. It was dark and deserted. Even the guards were nowhere in sight. Torches burned in the wall sconces, casting a feeble light that flickered and created shadows. A snorting, breathy sound came from a darkened corner of the room. The shadows swayed, dancing in a nonexistent breeze. Crossing the hall, I entered the corridor beyond. It was the corridor that led to my aunt's room, the corridor that had always led to safety.

Inside the doorway, I found myself in the cozy familiarity of my aunt's room. The fire burned brightly in the fireplace just as it always did. The drifting balls of witches' light cast their comforting glow just as they always did. But still, something didn't feel right.

I walked to the fireplace, my hands held toward the fire to warm the chill from my fingers. Then suddenly, everything was different. The room had changed. No longer in my aunt's safe, inviting room, I now stood by the fireplace in Vannabe's cottage. Bright, shiny objects lay on the table, drawing me to them. The air around me wavered as I moved across the floor. Reaching the table, I found knives made of brightly polished metal. The whisper of fabric came from behind me. I turned quickly.

Vannabe stood in the doorway, her heavy skirts swaying, a wide-bladed knife in her hand. "I won't keep you long," she said. "I only want your tongue and your toes. You know you'd do anything to help a friend. Think of me as your friend and let me have them. It's just a small favor. Tongue and toes, that's all I want." The whispering came again as Vannabe drew closer. "If you hold still, this won't hurt too much."

I woke with a start. My heart raced and my hands felt clammy. I felt disoriented and lost. My nest beneath the leaves was dark and confining. Panic-stricken, I pushed the leaves aside and scrambled into the open. I glanced around, trying to get my bearings. The back of my neck prickled the way it had when the eyeballs watched me. Vannabe was here! But when I looked up, it wasn't the witch who was swooping down on me, but an owl, its beak open in anticipation! Too scared to call out, too frightened to move, I pressed myself against the ground, convinced that I was about to die. Suddenly, a large, sinuous body whipped between us. Hissing, the snake lunged, barely missing the startled owl as it pulled up only inches from me. Its wings beating frantically, the owl fluttered away in distress, still alive.

"Are you all right?" hissed Fang, keeping his eyes on the departing owl.

"Yes," I breathed with a throat too dry from fear to say more.

"Go back to sleep," whispered Fang. "I will keep guard. You have nothing more to fear this night."

I surprised myself by believing him. If Fang had wanted to eat me, he wouldn't have waited this long. For the first time in days I began to feel secure. Burrowing under the leaves again, I thought of waking Eadric, of telling him how close I had come to being an owl's midnight snack. But the more I thought about it, the fewer reasons I could find for waking him, so I let him sleep undisturbed. *I'll tell him in the morning,* I thought. *There's no need to tell him now.*

Eadric was still asleep when I woke the next morning. I remembered my intention to tell him about the owl, but in the light of day I began to doubt that it had really happened. After eating a dozen salty mosquitoes, I went looking for a nice juicy beetle. When I returned, I found Eadric and Li'l in the midst of a heated discussion.

"Why didn't you wake me?" demanded Eadric. "I told you I would take the second watch."

"You told me you weren't going to sleep at all! I could hear you snoring all night long," Li'l said.

"Don't exaggerate! Frogs don't snore! Maybe your hearing isn't as good as I thought it was."

"Maybe not all frogs snore, but you do. I found myself a hidey-hole in the trunk of that tree and I could hear you even from there! It's a good thing nothing happened last night. If I could hear your snoring, other creatures could have as well. We're lucky no predators came to see what was making that awful racket."

"Good morning, Li'l, Eadric," I said, nodding to my friends. "Is everything all right?"

"Just fine and dandy," said Li'l, yawning broadly. "If you're ready, we should be off."

"I'll tell Fang," I said. "He's around here somewhere."

"Don't bother," said Li'l. "I already told him. Just follow this deer trail up the hill and over the other side. You'll be able to see the castle once you reach the road. I'm going to find myself a new hidey-hole at the edge of

131

the forest so I can take a nap. I'll see you when you get there. Your voices will wake me up. I have excellent hearing, remember?" Spreading her wings wide, she glared at Eadric. "And Eadric, next time I will wake you up, whether you want me to or not."

Li'l took off, leaving me to adjust the vial on Eadric's back. I untied the knot and straightened the twisted twine. "What happened back there between you and Li'l? She seemed pretty upset."

"What can I say? She's a bat with an attitude problem. I am feeling out of sorts, though. I had a terrible nightmare last night."

"What happened in your nightmare?"

"An owl almost got you. Thank goodness it was just a dream, Emma. I'd never forgive myself if anything ever happened to you."

Eadric looked so sincere that I almost felt sorry for him, except his mistake had put a life on the line, and the life had been mine. I pulled the twine tighter, then tried to tie a better knot. "It wasn't a dream, Eadric. There really was an owl and it really did almost get me. And Li'l was right. You do snore! If it hadn't been for Fang, I'd be filling some owl's stomach right now!"

Twelve

*E*adric and I hurried now; we could see the castle from the top of the hill and were eager to reach it. Farmland lay on both sides of the castle road almost as far as the gates. Behind the castle lay the swamp.

We had started down the hill and were passing one of the ancient oaks when we heard the angry buzzing of flies. Although we had both eaten before starting out that morning, Eadric was determined to investigate. I followed him, hoping that I could persuade him to come away. We found the flies along with a few scraps of fur and a scattering of grisly bones—all that was left of some unfortunate forest creature. The flies clustered on the remains, their black bodies glistening blue and green in the sunlight.

"Please don't stop now," I said to Eadric. "We've almost reached the road!"

Eadric smacked his lips, obviously more interested in catching flies than in anything I might have to say. "I'll only be a moment. Why don't you have some, too? There are plenty for both of us!"

"No, thank you," I said. "I'm not hungry." The thought of eating flies that had just crawled on carrion turned my stomach.

Unable to watch, I headed toward the road, hoping that Eadric would soon catch up. I had climbed halfway over a broken branch when something plucked me from the ground and flipped me over onto my back, squeezing the breath out of me. Screaming was impossible, for I didn't have enough air in my lungs to do more than grunt, but I kicked and thrashed about, frantically trying to free myself. Suddenly, I was flipped over again and found myself face-to-face with Fang. *Eadric was right!* I thought. *How could I have ever trusted a snake?*

Caught in the scaly coils, I was sure that I was looking at death itself when I noticed that the snake was no longer looking at me. Its eyes were fixed on something behind me, something that hissed and made the dead leaves rustle with its passing. The pressure on my body grew unbearable as the coils tightened. Then, in an instant, I was tossed aside like rubbish. I flew through the air and would have kept on going if I hadn't hit a tree, slid down the trunk, and landed on my back with my legs sticking up in the air. Partially stunned, I turned my head and looked back the way I'd come. Much to my surprise I realized that there were two Fangs, or at least two snakes that looked like Fang, coiled together in a silent battle. I tried to scoot backward, hoping that neither one would notice me. Writhing, the snakes twisted around until they were facing each other.

"Why, Fang, sweetie, is that you?" said a feminine voice. I noticed for the first time that the snake that spoke was smaller than the other, her body slimmer, her markings slightly different.

"Clarisse?" said the larger snake in a voice that I recognized as Fang's.

"Where have you been, lover boy? You've been gone an awfully long time."

"I was captured and imprisoned by a witch. We have only just escaped."

"We?"

"You attacked one of my companions. Emma," Fang said, raising his head to look at me, "this is Clarisse."

"Pleased to meet you, Emma," said the slimmer snake, delicately flicking her tongue in my direction. "Now, Fang, do you suppose you could let me go? I have a little unfinished business to attend to."

"As long as it doesn't include eating one of my friends."

"Any friend of yours is a friend of mine, and you know I never eat friends."

"Of course, Clarisse. My mistake." The snakes relaxed their coils and slid apart, although they didn't go far.

"Are you home to stay, Fang, or just passing through? The children are quite sizable now, and I know they would love to see their daddy."

"I have an obligation I must fulfill, but I shall return in a few days."

"Good!" said Clarisse. "It's almost that time of year again. Now, you make sure you come look me up as soon as you get back!"

"Rest assured, Clarisse, I intend to do just that."

"You take care now, Fang. I'll be seeing you later." She rubbed her head against Fang's in a gesture so tender that I felt embarrassed to be watching. Swiveling her head to look at me, she flicked her tongue in my direction once more. "It's been nice meeting you, Emma. Good luck with whatever it is you two are doing!"

Fang watched Clarisse slither off, his eyes glazing over as her tail disappeared in the leaf mold.

"Was that your wife?" I asked, wincing at the pain of bruised ribs.

He blinked and slowly turned to me as if he were coming out of a trance. "Unlike humans, snakes do not marry."

"Your girlfriend, then. Your mate, maybe."

"Perhaps one of those terms would apply."

"She's very pretty," I said. "For a snake."

"Actually, she is considered quite lovely."

"Hey, you two," called a voice, and Eadric appeared

from behind a tree. "I thought you would have reached the road by now. You should have stayed and tried the flies. They were delicious."

"Maybe I should have," I said, "considering what the alternative turned out to be."

It was already midmorning by the time we left the shade of the forest. Li'l was waiting for us just as she'd said she would, hanging upside down from the branch of a pear tree like an overripe piece of fruit. I could see the castle again from where I stood, the unmistakable towers rising above the countryside. With our destination seeming so close, I was determined to reach it before dark, although it would probably be a very long way to hop.

"You'll be leaving now, won't you?" Eadric asked Fang.

The snake shook his head ever so slightly. "Not yet. I shall go with you as far as the castle. When you have reached it safely, I shall return here to reclaim my territory and make my home."

"Have you ever been to the castle before?" I asked, proud of my own home and eager to hear some words of praise.

"No, although I know of some who have. You had best be careful when you get there. I hear the castle is a very dangerous place."

"Dangerous!" I said indignantly. "It's not dangerous at all! I've lived there all my life and I've never seen anything dangerous!"

"Of course not, for you were there as a human and a princess."

"Then you believed me when I told everyone at the cottage that I'm an enchanted princess and that Eadric is a prince? You all laughed, so I thought you doubted me."

"I do not know about the others, but I did not believe you until you read the spell. I do not know of any other frogs who can read."

"I believed her when she *said* she could read," Li'l said. "I've never met a creature who even claimed that before! Hey, everybody, see over there." She shaded her eyes with one wing and pointed with the other. "The road curves past those farms and ends at the castle gate. You're almost home, Emma."

"Thank goodness! And we'll be humans again as soon as we find my aunt!" I hopped onto the road, eager to leave. "I'll lead now. I know my way from here."

I was so excited that I couldn't hop the way I normally did. Instead, I jumped, leaped, and bounced down the road like a child's toy. My excitement must have been contagious, because Eadric tried to match his hops to mine while Fang slithered faster than we had ever seen him move before. Even Li'l was caught up in the excitement, flying loops in the sky above us until her wings began to tire. Panting at the unaccustomed exertion, she settled in an old apple tree by the side of the road and waited for us to catch up.

It wasn't long before Eadric discovered the anthills. He amused himself for an hour or so by taking samples from each one he found, but stopped after tasting a red ant. "They have too much bite," he told me, his mouth twisted in pain.

The road was warm and dry beneath our feet. Dust swirled around us as we hopped, coating our skin and making us cough. The air grew hotter as the day went on, and Eadric and I soon suffered the effects of the drying sun. After a while, feeling pinched and withered, we slowed to a halfhearted walk.

"I have to sit down," I finally told my friends. "I feel faint."

"Frogs aren't meant to be out of water for so long," panted Eadric. "We need to find a stream or a lake. Even a puddle will do."

"I shall ask Li'l to look around," said Fang, who never left our side for long.

I knew that talking to Fang made Li'l nervous, but she flew to us when he called to her and landed a good distance from him, listening to his request. After looking Eadric and me over and seeing the truth of Fang's words, she nodded and took off. I watched her circle and come back a short time later.

"I found a pond at the bottom of the hill," she said, landing beside me. She frowned when she saw Eadric sprawled on the dirt road. "What's wrong with him?"

"He's passed out," I told her, "and I don't feel well, either."

"We need your help, Li'l," said Fang. "I cannot carry him, so it is up to you."

"Me?" squeaked the bat. "I've never lifted anything that big before!"

"You lifted the books in Vannabe's cottage when you brought them to me," I said.

"It's more like I dropped them. Oh, all right. I'll try to carry him," said Li'l, "but I don't think I can for long. He's a big boy, isn't he?"

"Emma, are you well enough to walk?" asked Fang.

I tried to stand, but my legs buckled under me.

"Here," said Fang. "Climb onto my back. I can take you there if you can hold on."

"Ugh!" Li'l grunted, struggling to lift Eadric. "I'm going to get a hernia! This frog needs to start eating fat-free insects!"

Just beyond the next rise, the ground sloped away from the road. A pond lay at the bottom, a welcome sight for everyone. Li'l half carried, half dragged Eadric up the hill. When she reached the top, she lost her grip and his limp body slid down the other side.

"Look out below!" shouted Li'l. She took to the air

and flew after him, but he hit a bump and began to tumble head over heels over vial of dragon's breath. Finally, Eadric plopped into the water and Li'l flew off in search of a shady tree, her job done.

The pond was all we could have hoped for. It was close. It was cool. It was wet. I clung to Fang's back all the way down the hill, although I felt weak and nauseous and had a hard time concentrating. When he reached the bottom, Fang wriggled into the shallow water long enough for me to slide off. He stayed by the edge to make sure that I was all right, but as soon as I began to move around he slithered back up the hill and onto a large flat rock overlooking the pond.

I lay in the shallows until I started to feel like myself again. When I was able to, I swam toward Eadric, who still lay sprawled in the water where he had landed when he fell. I was concerned about him: his face looked pasty and his skin was too warm. He muttered when I laid my hand on his forehead, but his eyes remained closed. Taking his hand in mine, I waited until he twitched and opened his eyes before I turned and plunged into the depths of the pond. Eadric soon followed me, his feeble strokes becoming powerful scissor kicks as he regained his strength.

The water felt wonderful! We somersaulted and dove, we floated and twirled, and all the while our skin let water into our parched flesh. I thought of the day I had learned to swim and of how much else I had learned since then.

I was enjoying the water and the breeze that ruffled the surface of the pond when suddenly something grabbed my foot and pulled me under. Kicking hard, I shook Eadric's hand loose and popped to the surface like a cork. I was still laughing when Eadric followed me up, his face appearing only inches from mine.

"You know something?" he said, grinning. "You're a much better swimmer than you used to be. It won't be long before you're almost as good as I am."

"Is that so? And how do you think I'm doing in my other froggy skills?"

"Your hopping is good, but you still need to work on catching insects."

"Really? Well, I don't think I'll ever be able to eat as well as you can."

Eadric smiled smugly. I patted him on the shoulder, then did a flip in the water and swam away before he could see my own smile.

Thirteen

With Li'l leading the way and Fang guarding us from behind, we were soon back on the road to the castle. Mumbling her apologies, Li'l flew to the first tree she could find. When we reached the tree, Fang pointed out her darker shape amidst the leafy shade. "Li'l," he hissed loudly, "we are here."

"Go on without me," called back a tired voice. "I'll catch up later. I need to sleep a little longer."

"We'll meet you at the castle," I shouted. "Look for us by the drawbridge."

Li'l didn't answer. With a sleepy sigh, she'd already dozed off again.

"I hope she heard me," I said to Fang and Eadric as we continued down the road.

"She is a bat," said Fang. "I am sure she heard you. However, bats traditionally sleep during daylight hours and we have asked much of her today. She is also more timid than I expected now that she is out of her element, and I fear that she will be easily frightened for some time to come. I believe her bossy manner was a cover for her insecurities."

Late that afternoon, a farm wagon leaving the castle grounds rumbled down the road. Fang moved off into the grass while Eadric and I patiently waited for the wagon to pass. I was shielding my eyes from the cloud of dust when a young boy walking beside the wagon spotted us. "Look, Father," he called. "Frogs! I'm going to catch them!"

"Now, Robbie," said the farmer, "why don't you leave them where they are? You take them home and they'll die like the last ones."

"But I want to play with them," the boy insisted.

Eadric and I had heard the child and had no intention of letting him catch us. I hustled Eadric off the side of the road, following Fang into the tall grass. The boy, who had seen us go, ran over with a stick in his hand. "I know you're in there," he said, squatting on his heels. "Come out here where I can see you." The long stick jabbed the grass, narrowly missing us.

Eadric, trying to frighten the boy away by making himself look big and intimidating, straightened his legs and arms and put on his fiercest expression. Since his legs were longer than his arms, his back end stuck up higher in the air, forcing him to tilt his head back to look at the boy. With the vial of dragon's breath still strapped to him, Eadric looked like a bizarre multicolored hunchback, and I would have laughed if I hadn't been so frightened. Because he was in front of Fang, Eadric couldn't see the snake raise his head above the grass and glare at the boy through slitted eyes. Fang hissed softly and the boy nearly fell over his own feet trying to get back to his father's wagon.

"Did you see that?" said Eadric proudly. "I scared him off! He'll think twice before coming after a frog again, won't he!"

"I'm sure you're right," I said. "Especially one who travels with a snake. Next time he might even stay in the wagon."

With the farm wagon and the boy gone, we returned to the road. The rosy glow of the sunset outlined the castle and made it seem all the more inviting. However, we had gone only a short distance when we felt the vibration of approaching vehicles. Soon, two more farm wagons and a tinker's cart passed by. Petitioners from the village who had stayed late at court followed in a carriage. With so much traffic on the road, we decided that it was no longer safe and moved off into the fields.

Traveling across the uneven ground was slower than it had been on the hard-packed dirt, and night fell before we reached the castle. The drawbridge was already up. It wouldn't be lowered again until morning.

We were seated in the dust at the end of the road when Li'l flew down to land beside us. "There you are!" she said. "I've been looking all over for you! I don't like it out here. It's too open and there's too much going on. I think I saw a hawk, although I'm not real sure. So where are we going now, Emma? Do you have any good hidey-holes in that castle of yours?"

"I'm sure you'll find plenty of places to hide," I assured her, "but why don't you go see if you can find my aunt first? That's her tower, the tall one on the left. She said she would be away for a few days, but she should be back by now."

"What about you? Are you going straight there?"

"We have to get inside the castle," I explained, "and the drawbridge is up."

"Why's that a problem?" Li'l asked. "You're frogs. You can swim across the moat. I'll go up to the tower and take a peek inside. Now, you're sure your aunt won't mind?"

"She won't mind at all. Go on ahead. We'll be there as soon as we can." I watched Li'l become a dark speck as she flew over the moat. When I could no longer see her in the gloom, I turned and spoke to Fang. "And what about you, Fang? Are you coming with us?"

"No, I must return home now. I have much work to do to reestablish my territory."

"Thank you for being there all those times," I said,

throwing my arms around him. "You were right—we did need you."

"I know. And you are welcome." My hug made him uncomfortable, for he quickly backed away, eyeing me warily. "Emma," he said, "because of your emotional demonstration, I must tell you something that I would not otherwise have disclosed."

"You can tell me anything, Fang. If anyone has the right, it's you."

"I understand that humans whose lives have been saved may feel a certain ... affection for their rescuers. If you are feeling such an affinity for me, you must know that my heart is engaged elsewhere."

If he thought that I had a crush on him ... I tried not to laugh, and thought of a trick I'd learned when my mother caught me in a giddy mood and I knew she would disapprove if I laughed out loud. I had only to think of something sad, such as the death of my first puppy, to make myself lose the desire to laugh. I tried it now and it worked, allowing me to alter my expression to one more suitable to a jilted female.

"Is it Clarisse?" I asked, looking as mournful as I could.

"Yes," he said, nodding solemnly. "You are not too badly disappointed, are you?"

"I'll recover, but it won't be easy."

"Good luck in your endeavors. And the same goes

147

for you, Eadric."

"Thanks, Fang. It was ... an experience having you along."

I watched Fang slither down the road with mixed emotions. He was a snake and I had always been terrified of snakes. Because I was now a frog, he should have been one of my worst enemies, yet he had proven to be a friend, someone I could trust when I was in danger.

"What did you mean when you thanked Fang like that?" Eadric demanded. "He didn't do anything! And who is Clarisse?"

"And *you* accused *me* of being unobservant! Never mind, Eadric. Maybe I'll tell you about it one day. Let's just say that he was a much better companion than either of us thought he would be."

"I guess that's true," said Eadric. "At least he didn't eat us."

Fourteen

Following Eadric to the edge of the moat, I peered down into the water, thinking about how often I'd passed by without really looking at it. The moat had been a fixture, part of the castle fortifications that I knew we needed, but it had never seemed particularly important. I'd certainly never considered swimming in it before.

A breeze blew past, carrying the stench of decaying garbage. "Pew!" I said, wrinkling my nose. "Do you smell that? Is that the water?"

Eadric lowered his head and sniffed. "It sure is."

I stepped back from the edge, my stomach churning. Having grown up near the moat, I suppose I'd been used to the smell. Maybe it was because of my enhanced frog senses, or maybe the moat had gotten stinkier since I'd been gone, but for whatever reason, I now found the stench overwhelming. "I'm not swimming in anything that smells that bad!" I said.

"We don't have much of a choice, do we?"

"We could wait until morning when they lower the drawbridge."

"But then all the wagons and foot traffic will be going in," Eadric said, shaking his head. "Crossing the moat is probably the best idea. Just keep your mouth closed and swim as fast as you can."

I looked at the moonlight's reflection on the moat. The other bank suddenly seemed so far away, so high above the water. "I don't think I can do this!"

"Sure you can!" said Eadric. "You just need a positive attitude!"

"Fine! I'm positive I can't do this!"

Eadric sighed. "You're right. You can't do it if you don't believe you can. But don't imagine yourself failing—imagine yourself doing it. Picture yourself swimming across and climbing up the other side. I know you can do it if you really want to."

I closed my eyes and tried to picture myself swimming through cool, clear water, speeding to the opposite side of the moat and climbing the stones as if I'd done it every day of my life. Unfortunately, I could still smell the water, and the illusion was hard to maintain. It was easier to imagine Eadric swimming beside me, holding his nose with one hand and paddling with the other, saying, "Picture yourself as a bubble, floating across the water," his voice fading as he disappeared in a stinky green fog.

I giggled. "Now, *that* I can believe!" I said under my breath as I slipped into the moat.

I tried to breathe as little as possible, but it wasn't easy. The cold, greasy water made me gasp, and I gagged when it almost got in my mouth. Holding my head as high as I could, I tried to keep my face dry. A large glob of something soft and sticky bumped into me and I shuddered with disgust. *Thank goodness it's dark and I can't see what that was,* I thought.

"Emma, hurry up," said Eadric. "I think there's something in here with us."

"There sure is," I agreed. "There's all sorts of garbage floating in this water. This is disgusting!"

"No, I mean something alive. I just felt something swim past my feet."

A small wave nudged me forward, carrying me closer to the side of the moat. "Eadric," I whispered, suddenly afraid to talk out loud, "did you feel that? What could have made that wave?"

"Something bigger than a frog!" Eadric whispered back. "Here it comes again. Hurry, Emma, we're almost there!"

With the dry ground edging the moat only feet away, the castle loomed over us forbiddingly. Although I had always loved my home, I had never seen it from the moat before. Now I wished I never had. I kicked as hard as I could, arrowing through the water, and almost bumped into the fish. It was a small fish, only half as big as I was, but it startled me just the same. Its eyes were red and watery and swollen. It looked as though a third eye had begun to form between the first two, a shrunken eye that rattled loosely in its socket. Something brushed against my feet, but when I looked, the fish was still keeping pace with me. Evidently, the deformed little fish wasn't the only creature that lived in the moat.

When I finally bumped into the stone wall, I reached up and touched it with my hand. Eadric, who had already climbed out of the water, grasped my wrist and began to pull me up.

"Hurry!" said Eadric. "There's something in the water behind you!"

I looked down. Reflected in the light of the rising moon, a large silvery back arced above the water, heading toward me. Terror lent me the strength I needed. Digging my toes into the crumbling stone lining the moat, I fairly flew up the side and fell into Eadric's arms, knocking him off his feet. Something slapped the surface of the moat, splashing us with a wave of fetid water. Without looking back, we scrambled to safety as far from the moat as we could get.

"Now what?" I asked, wiping the moisture from my face with the back of my hand. Standing on the narrow stone ledge, I still felt exposed to whatever lived in the moat.

"Find a way in, I suppose. There has to be a hole or a missing stone or something we can use to get inside. We just have to look until we find it."

"And what if there isn't?"

"Then we wait until they open the door in the morning. Don't worry, I grew up in a castle, too, remember? Little boys explore everything. I found hundreds of chinks in the walls of my parents' castle, places too small for a little boy but certainly large enough for a couple of frogs. If anyone can find a way into your castle, it's me."

The moon was high overhead when we finally found an opening. Although it never grew any wider, it extended far back through the castle wall, forming a cramped, dark tunnel. Dried rodent droppings and beetle casings littered the floor, telling the tale of those who had passed that way before. The air was dank and smelled musty, but it was a way in and I was thrilled that we had found it.

The tunnel ended abruptly at a large open space. I was disoriented until I realized that we had reached the Great Hall, the heart of the castle and the most important room. A warren of corridors and lesser chambers led from the hall, making it the focal point of the entire building. The remains of a fire burned in the massive stone fireplace, and my father's dogs lay twitching in their sleep on the hearth, their bellies filled with table scraps.

"This is wonderful!" I whispered into Eadric's

eardrum. "We don't have far to go now. The stairs leading to my aunt's rooms are at the end of that corridor."

"What about the dogs?"

"We'll have to be careful not to wake them, that's all." Eadric looked skeptical, but I was insistent. "Eadric," I said, "we have to go now. It will be so busy here in the morning that it will be impossible to pass through then. If we don't go now, we might as well turn around and go back to the swamp."

"I can't help it—I don't like dogs. And look at the size of those monsters! Are you sure they're all asleep?"

"Of course I'm sure. Can't you hear them snoring? Here, I'll go first. Just stay close and be as quiet as you can."

I hopped once, but the slap of my feet on the stone floor echoed throughout the Great Hall. I froze and listened to the dogs. Their moans, whimpers, snores, and slow breathing assured me that they still slept. One dog growled in its sleep while another ran, its legs twitching, its body never leaving the floor. My father's biggest hound, Bowser, no longer a duckling, lay on his back with his legs in the air, flapping away as if he were trying to fly. I decided that Grassina must have finally found the right parchment to restore Bowser's dogness.

When there was no change in the rhythm of their breathing, I began to hop again, stopping every now and then to listen. We had reached the far wall and had only

154

a little farther to go when I hopped into a puddle of dog pee, splashing myself with the smelly fluid from head to toe. "Oh, yuck!" I said, forgetting the need for silence.

My head whipped around when I heard one of the dogs begin to stir. It was Bowser. Blearily stumbling to his feet, the big hound lurched in our direction.

"Quick, in here!" said Eadric, pointing to a wooden bucket. Although the bucket was familiar, I couldn't remember what it was normally used for, but with Bowser on his way we didn't have time to be picky.

"One, two, three, jump!" I said and we both leaped over the edge and into tepid water. "Eadric!" I whispered as it dawned on me where we were. "This is the dogs' water! What if he's coming to get a drink?"

"Why didn't you tell me?"

"I just realized—"

"Shh! Here he comes!"

I shrank against the side of the bucket as Bowser's great head came into view. *The dog is half asleep,* I thought, *so maybe he won't notice.* I knew the moment that Bowser sensed us, for his ears pricked up. His rank breath washed over me as he looked into the bucket. When I saw Eadric swim to the bottom, I knew that it was up to me.

"Quack!" I said, sounding as much like a duck as I could. "Quack! Quack! Quack!"

"What the ..." Bowser jerked his head back in surprise.

"Quack! Quack! Quack!" I said again, bobbing up and down in the water like a duck.

"Oh, no, another one!" whined Bowser as he backed away.

Although I could no longer see him, I could hear his claws scrabbling on the stone floor as he scurried out of the hall. Eadric was still underwater when I decided that it was safe to go. Sighing, I reached down and pulled him to the surface. "The dog is gone," I said. "We can get out now."

"I guess it was too dark for him to see us under the water," Eadric said, boosting himself onto the rim of the bucket.

I slid over the edge and plopped onto the floor. "Or maybe he's afraid of ducks."

"Why would you keep ducks in your Great Hall?"

"I never said we did."

Turning to look behind us, Eadric scratched his head with his toe, and I heard him mumble softly, "But I thought you said ..."

After trying so hard to be quiet in the Great Hall, entering the corridor was a relief. "I'll race you!" I whispered, eager to stretch my muscles.

"You don't stand a chance, slowpoke!" Eadric whispered back.

We raced across the floor, extending our legs in long, bounding leaps. Arrow slits in the tower walls let in the moonlight, making the steps easy to see. We hopped up one pie-slice-shaped step after another, racing to see who would reach the top first. Eadric won even though he was still wearing the vial of dragon's breath, landing on the top step seconds before me.

When I reached the landing, I was panting and tired but happier than I'd been in a long time. "You won," I said, trying to catch my breath, "only because you have longer legs than I do."

"That's not it at all," he said, panting just as heavily. "I won because I'm a superior hopper and you are a slowpoke."

"It doesn't matter—we're here now!" I grinned so hard my face hurt. "With my aunt Grassina's help, we'll be humans again in no time!"

Fifteen

I had raised my hand to knock on Grassina's door when Eadric waved me back. "Before you get your aunt, there's something I've been wanting to say," he said, avoiding my eyes. "I know I'll be happy to be a prince again, but there's a lot about being a frog that I've really enjoyed, especially since you became one, too."

"What do you mean?" I asked.

"Just that ... Oh, never mind. Go ahead, knock on the door." Eadric turned his face away, but not before I saw a frown creasing his forehead.

"In a minute. First tell me what you mean."

Eadric sighed. "I shouldn't have said anything. It's just that being a frog with you has been fun. Even the bad parts were better with you than when I was a frog by myself. As far as I'm concerned, it wouldn't be so awful if we had to stay frogs, not if we were together." Eadric finished in a rush, as if he wouldn't finish at all if he didn't hurry. He cleared his throat, then added, "And you'd never have to marry Jorge."

"I don't know what to say." I reached out to him, but he pulled away from me and turned to the door.

"You don't have to say anything," he said stiffly. "Go ahead and knock."

I'd seen the stubborn look on his face and knew that it was useless to try to question him. Not quite understanding what he meant, I could feel my excitement deflate. After all we'd gone through, did he want to remain a frog? Did he want me to remain a frog, too? I shrugged and lifted my hand to knock, determined to ask Eadric about it later. Before my hand touched the door, it was flung open and my aunt Grassina rushed onto the landing.

"Emma!" she called, her lips quirking at the corners. She turned her head, looking for some sign of me, but she never looked down to see two frogs waiting by her feet. Her smile faded, and she fumbled for the door behind her. "I could have sworn ... ," she said to herself.

"Aunt Grassina, I'm down here!" I shouted, thrilled at finally seeing her again. *Now everything will work out,* I thought. *Aunt Grassina can take care of anything.* But my heart sank as Grassina looked down and, seeing only two frogs at her door, turned to go back inside. The sorrow in her eyes made my heart tighten. I couldn't stand to see her look so sad.

"It's me," I shouted, hopping up and down in

frustration. "It's me, it's me, it's me! It's your niece, Emma! I've been turned into a frog! Look at me, Aunt Grassina! Please look at me!"

When Grassina looked down, the stricken expression on her face almost made me cry. "It's not possible," she said. "I gave my niece a talisman to protect her from such spells. You can't be my Emma."

"But I am! I kissed an enchanted prince—Eadric, here—and turned into a frog!"

Grassina raised one eyebrow. "I suppose that could have happened if something went wrong with the talisman," she said slowly. "Emma did ask me about talking frogs and it would certainly explain her disappearance. Perhaps you two should come in."

We didn't need a second invitation. Eadric and I followed my aunt, nearly hopping on the hem of her gown in our hurry to enter the room. Even from a frog's point of view, the room was lovely. The rosy glow from the witches' lights made everything look warm and appealing. Sinking up to my knees in the soft rugs, I reveled in the way they cushioned my tired feet. I sank down on the rug in front of the fireplace and stretched out my legs. Eadric followed me to the rug without ever taking his eyes off Grassina.

"So that's your aunt, huh?" said Eadric under his breath. "She's quite a looker! She's a much better dresser than Vannabe or the old witch, too. She even smells better."

"Thank you," said Grassina, whose hearing had always been good. "I suppose I should take that as a compliment. Just who are Vannabe and the old witch?"

"The old witch was named Mudine," I said. "She lived in the forest, but she died a year ago. Vannabe wants to be a witch. She took over Mudine's house and books when Mudine died."

"I see," said Grassina. "That's too bad. Mudine was a talented witch in her day."

"Did you know her?" asked Eadric. "She was the one who turned me into a frog."

"Is that so?" said Grassina. "Then she can't really be dead, can she? If she had died, the spell would have been broken as well."

"So what do you think happened to her?" I asked. "We were told that she was sick. She lay down on her bed and disappeared in a puff of smoke."

"She may have gone somewhere for a rest. Or if she were very sick, she may have gone to see a witch doctor. Sometimes their cures take a long time to work."

"Maybe Grandmother knows what happened to her," I said. "The old witches sit around a bonfire and trade stories and recipes on Wednesday nights. She might have heard something about Mudine."

"Where does your grandmother live?" asked Eadric.

"In the Old Witches' Retirement Community. It's a very nice place where every witch gets to choose her own

161

cottage. My grandmother's is made of gingerbread, but I think she's sorry she picked it. She's always complaining that children from the village are eating her out of house and home. I'm sorry she didn't get the one her neighbor has. It has chicken legs and can walk around."

"I've never heard of this place. Where is it?"

"Over the river and through the woods. It's easy to find. Even my horse knows the way."

"Well, Eadric," said Grassina, obviously becoming impatient, "regardless of what happened to Mudine, she did a good job when she transformed you. You are a very handsome frog."

Eadric beamed and ran his hand over his smooth green scalp as if brushing back nonexistent hair. I had never realized that a frog could look so vain.

"And what is that vial you're wearing on your back?" asked Grassina. "It looks like aged dragon's breath, if I'm not mistaken."

Reaching behind him, Eadric patted the vial and nodded. "It's a little something I picked up in Vannabe's cottage. Didn't want to leave it there for her to misuse."

"Very good thinking, Eadric. Leaving it for someone who doesn't know what she's doing would have been a terrible idea."

Eadric's smile was so smug it was sickening.

Grassina turned and looked me in the eye. "And as for you, you seem to know quite a bit about Emma's grandmother. You really want me to believe that you're my niece, Emma, don't you?"

"But I am Emma!"

"All right then, tell me why I should believe you. Let me hear your story so I can make up my mind." Grassina gently picked us up and carried us to a small table. Wings folded, the glass butterflies rested on the crystalline blossoms. I made myself comfortable beneath the nodding bloom of a large amethyst-colored rose. Eadric sat beside me, eyes wide as he realized that the flowers and butterflies were alive.

Sitting back in her chair, my aunt waited for me to begin.

"Where should I start?" I asked.

"Start with the day you became a frog."

"It's a long story," I warned.

"I'm in no hurry."

"Well," I began, "it was the day Prince Jorge came to visit. . . ."

I have always been a thorough storyteller. I left out no details, including many that Grassina could have done without. Eadric fell asleep halfway through the story. Grassina, however, seemed to be captivated. She scowled when I told her about Vannabe's treatment of the animals, and she laughed when I told her about the way the fireflies lit up Eadric's throat. She interrupted me only once, when she got up to get herself a cup of tea and a saucer of water for me. My throat was sore by the time I finally finished talking.

"Wonderful story!" said Grassina. "Very entertaining! But anyone with a little imagination could have made it up. Tell me why I should believe that you are my niece. I need some sort of proof, something that you can't have overheard and is specific to Emma."

There was a rustling at the window and a black shape darted into the room. It flew behind Grassina's chair and cowered under the seat. "Tickle her!" said a voice. "Or tell her a really funny joke."

"What was that?" Grassina said, jumping to her feet.

"That's Li'l. I told you about her."

"Ah, yes, the witch's bat." Grassina crouched beside her chair and peered at the bat clinging to the underside of the seat. "So, Li'l, you think you might be interested in living here?"

"That depends. Are you a real witch or a pretender like Vannabe?"

"Oh, I'm a real witch all right. Just ask Emma's mother."

"Do you practice magic much?"

"I not only practice it, I do it! So, did I pass the test?"

"I guess, but there's still a problem. You don't have any rafters. Where's a bat to hang out without rafters?"

"Hmmm, rafters. I hadn't thought of that." Grassina tilted her head to look up at the ceiling. The witches' lights bobbed in the gentle breeze blowing through the window. "And I have all those lights, too. Don't worry, I'm sure we'll think of something. But what did you mean when you suggested that we tickle the frog?"

"Tickle her and you'll see."

Eadric had woken shortly before the end of the story. "I will!" he said, reaching for me.

"I don't know about this," I said, backing away from Eadric. "I don't like being tickled."

"It's for a good cause," he said, grabbing my arm with one hand and tickling me with the other. He tickled my neck. He tickled my sides. He tried to tickle under my arms, but I squirmed away, bumping into the vase. A pale pink rose quivered, dropping loose petals, which landed on the table with a *chink chink chink*.

Eadric grabbed my foot and sat down to tickle it.

"No!" I shouted. "Not that!" And that's when I began to laugh. I laughed until my sides hurt. I laughed until tears ran down my cheeks. I laughed until I was weak and gasping for breath. And my laughter didn't sound like the tinkling of bells. It was full-blown guffaws, belly laughs that started deep inside of me and erupted out of my mouth.

"Emma!" said the Green Witch, and she began to laugh, too. "Only my Emma laughs like that! It has to be true!"

"Stop! Stop!" I gasped, too weak to push Eadric away. Grinning, he let go of my foot and collapsed on the table.

"Tell me," he said, craning his neck to look at my aunt, "wouldn't there have been an easier way? Don't you have any magic powder or a spell to help you see who she really is?"

"Yes, I do, and I believe I'll use it now. There's something I want Emma to see.... Emma, you stand over here," she said, picking me up and setting me on the floor. "Eadric, you'd better step back. You don't want to be caught in the backwash."

Li'l peeked out from under the seat, her interest in magic greater than her fear of strangers. "Are you going to do magic now?"

"Yes, I am. Would you like to help me?"

"Oh, would I!" Li'l scurried across the floor to Grassina's side, gazing up at her with awe. "Mudine never let me do anything—except catch bugs, that is!"

Grassina nodded in understanding. "I see," she said. "But things will be different here." She turned and looked about, her eyes finally settling on an old candle stub resting in a congealed puddle of melted wax atop her worktable. With a whispered word and a flick of her finger, Grassina lit the candle. "Now, when I tell you, blow out that flame. But don't do it until I tell you to, understand?"

"Yes, ma'am," said Li'l. "I understand perfectly! Blow out that flame when you tell me to and not before! Yes, ma'am." Her eyes glittering with excitement, Li'l fluttered to the table, landing between a rolled parchment and the candle. Keeping her eyes on Grassina's face, Li'l puffed out her cheeks and held her breath.

"I do like enthusiasm," Grassina leaned down to whisper to me. "But we'd better hurry and get started before she passes out." Raising her arm, she pointed her finger at me and said, "Li'l, now!"

It took the little bat three puffs to blow out the candle, but when she finally did, the whole room suddenly went dark, darker than it had been before the candle was lit, since even the witches' lights had gone out. "How was that?" Li'l said, sounding pleased with herself.

Grassina spoke and her voice was sweet and clear.

Beyond the charm,
Beyond the spell,
Show us the truth
You know so well.

Discard the false
And let us see
Your real form
As it should be.

A shower of sparkles swept through the room, swirling around me like powdery snow caught in a sudden draft. They tickled my nose and I sneezed, squeezing my eyes shut. When I opened them, I could see myself standing above me, or at least that's the way it seemed. Where it had been dark only a moment before, the air now glowed with a diffuse light, showing my normal young-girl body standing with feet squarely planted where I still squatted on the floor. It was a bit disconcerting at first, until I realized that I could see through the image. Although no more solid than fine mist, my body looked natural except for the sparkles. At first I thought they were part of Grassina's spell, but they lingered, twinkling like a thousand fireflies around my image.

"What are those sparkles?" I asked.

Grassina turned to Li'l, who was hopping about on the table, her wings quivering with excitement. "I think Li'l can answer that, can't you, Li'l?"

Li'l bobbed up and down, too agitated to hold still. "She's got the touch, doesn't she? She's got the special flair that Mudine always talked about!"

"What does she mean, *flair?*" I asked.

"She means that you have a talent for magic," said Grassina. "It's a special gift and you have to be born with it. From what you've told me, Vannabe doesn't have it, but whether you want it or not, you do."

"I knew she did!" chimed in Li'l. "It took more than just being able to read to make those spells work so fast! You should have seen it. One minute those cages were locked tighter than a fat dog's collar, then she read that spell and wham! We were out of there! Mudine's spells never worked half that fast!"

Even after I'd worked the spells from Mudine's old books, I'd thought they had succeeded only because they were foolproof. I stood dumbly staring at my image with my mouth gaping like a dying fish. Maybe I really was meant to be a witch. Maybe, if I worked hard enough at it, I could come up with a spell that would rid me of my clumsiness. And maybe I could help other people as well! Grassina herself was always doing just that.

Grassina gestured broadly and the witches' lights glowed again, brightening the room and dissolving my already-thinning image. Her glance fell on me and her lips softened once more. "It's so good to have you back, Emma. I'd hug you, but I'm afraid I'd squash you flat."

"I'll wait," I said, relieved at her restraint.

"How do you like being a frog?"

"It has its moments. But that's what we want to talk to you about. We need you to turn us back into humans. Can you do it tonight or do you have to get ready first?"

"It's not that easy, I'm afraid. We have to determine why you became a frog. You say you kissed Eadric?"

I nodded. "It wasn't a very big kiss, either."

"Hmm," my aunt said, thinking hard. "Was there anyone else present when it happened?"

"No, we were alone."

"What were you wearing that day?"

169

"I had on my blue gown and my third-best shoes and my hair was—"

"No, I mean what jewelry did you have on? Do you remember?"

"Nothing, really, just the bracelet you gave me."

"Do you mean the charm reversal bracelet I gave you when you were five?"

"Charm *reversal* bracelet? So it wasn't just a pretty bracelet that glowed in the dark!"

"That bracelet had a special magic of its own. I gave it to you when you were just a little girl to protect you. Any witch who tried to cast a spell on you would find that same spell bouncing back onto her. But if you had that on when you kissed Eadric ..."

"I did," I said, nodding.

"Then that may be the answer. You see, the spell wasn't being cast on you."

"So when Eadric and I kissed ..."

"The bracelet reversed the charm. Kissing Eadric was supposed to turn him back into a human, but instead the reverse happened and you turned into a frog. That should be easy to fix. All you need to do is put on the bracelet and kiss Eadric again. If you do that, you'll both revert to your human forms."

I should have been happy that we knew what had caused my transformation, but I was disappointed that the solution wasn't going to be easier. When I noticed that my aunt was watching me, I frowned and began to fidget.

"You do know where the bracelet is, don't you, Emma?" asked Grassina.

"Sort of," I said reluctantly. "We saw an otter swim away with it. I guess we have to find him ... unless you can do something about it. Can't you undo the spell with one of your own?"

"Certainly, if I had cast the spell in the first place. But I didn't, so you are the only one who can reverse it. However, I might be able to help you find the otter.... Eadric, you look troubled. Is something wrong?"

"Not really," he said. "It's just that every time I think I'm going to become a prince again, something happens. Maybe I'm supposed to live out the rest of my life as a frog."

"You can if you want to, but then Emma will remain a frog as well. Your spells are linked now, so you either both remain frogs or you both turn back into humans."

"I vote for the human," I said, remembering how often my life had been in danger as a frog.

"Then I do, too," said Eadric. He sighed and scratched the back of his head with his toe. "I don't suppose you know anyone who is going toward the swamp tomorrow, do you?"

"I'll take you there myself. It isn't every day that I get to carry a prince and a princess in a basket!"

171

Sixteen

With dawn still hours away, we decided to get as much sleep as we could before heading for the swamp. Eadric was already snoring softly on a cushioned chair when Grassina bent down to say good night. "Sleep well, Emma. It may take longer than you expect to find the bracelet. I want you to have your wits about you so you'll come back in one piece. I don't know what I'm going to tell your parents about this."

"Don't tell them anything," I said. "I'll talk to them myself when we get back." I had no idea what I would tell them, but I knew that I had a lot to say. I was pleased when I realized that the thought of confronting my parents didn't make me nervous the way it would have before.

"Good!" Grassina said, sounding satisfied. "I knew that sooner or later you would handle these things your-self. But I must tell you that your mother misses you more than you might think. When she first realized you were gone, she had everyone in the castle out looking for you. She isn't a bad person, you know. In fact, when we were younger, she was rumored to be the nicer sister."

"That must have been hard on you."

Grassina chuckled. "But it was true! I was the one with the magic, you see, and I was always getting into trouble. We knew from our earliest childhood who had the gift and who didn't. It wasn't fair to your mother, of course. She was left out of so many things. But in the end it wasn't fair to me, either, for your grandmother favored me and rejected my only suitor for not being good enough, whereas Chartreuse was free to marry whomever she chose."

"You mean to say that she *chose* Father? I thought it was an arranged marriage."

"If it was arranged, she did it herself."

"Did my mother resent you?" I asked.

"Of course she did! I was the favorite child, after all. I think that's why she's been so hard on you. We're so much alike, you and I."

⟡

We took short naps and woke just before dawn. Grassina lined a wicker basket with soft cloths, placed a small fruit tart on the bottom, then set it on the floor. "I know fruit tart isn't normally part of a frog's diet, but I thought you might be hungry, and I'm out of insects."

Eadric promptly crawled into the basket and flicked his tongue toward the tart.

"This is wonderful!" he announced, settling down to devour the rest.

I followed him, too excited to eat. "Isn't this great, Eadric?" I said as Grassina lifted the basket. "We'll find the otter, get the bracelet, and I'll kiss you. We can be back in time for lunch, dinner at the latest."

"I'd be less worried if I were doing it as a human," grumbled Eadric.

Grassina carried the basket down the stairs and through the Great Hall. The dogs were awake, begging for scraps and getting under the servants' feet. Bowser took one look at my aunt and scurried under the table, but three other dogs came to investigate the basket, nudging it with their noses and whining to see inside. The wonderful smells of fruit tart and frog were more than they could resist. Grassina shooed them away, but they were persistent and followed her to the door. I crouched in the bottom of the basket with my eyes tightly shut, as if that would protect me from the dogs. Eadric was so engrossed in eating his fruit tart that he never noticed anything.

Once through the garden, I gave Grassina directions to the pond where I had met Eadric. While Eadric finished off the tart, I peered over the edge of the basket and watched the world go by. Little had changed since I last saw the pond. A wood duck had left its webbed foot-prints in the mud. A queen bee had started a new hive in the old hollow tree at the edge of the pond. Nothing looked as big and scary from up high. I began to feel as though I could handle anything.

"Now, where did this kiss take place?" Grassina asked. "We need to be fairly precise, so try to remember."

I pointed to a bare spot by the edge of the pond where nothing seemed to grow. "Right over there!"

"Are you sure?" said Eadric, leaning over the side of the basket for a better look.

"Of course I'm sure! It was my first kiss! I remember everything about it … at least until things went fuzzy."

"Fine!" said Grassina, catching Eadric as he started to tumble out of the basket, overbalanced by the vial he still wore. "Then you two sit right here and we'll see if we can find that otter."

After setting the basket on an old stump, Grassina took something shiny and black out of the pouch attached to her gown. Light glinted off its sharp angles and flat surfaces the same way it did off one of my father's highly polished swords.

"Where did you get that?" I asked. I had never seen it before and I thought I was familiar with most of the tools my aunt used for her magic.

"While I was on that trip last week, I did a small

favor for a dragon. He gave me one of his scales to show his appreciation. Dragons are known for having an unerring sense of direction, so I thought this might come in handy. Now watch this...."

Holding the scale at arm's length, Grassina stepped to the spot I'd shown her and said,

> A golden bracelet rich with charms
> Fell to this soggy ground.
> An otter chanced upon it here
> And took what he had found.
>
> The rightful owner wants it back,
> She seeks the otter so
> She can retrieve that which is hers.
> Please tell her where to go.

Although the scale remained black as coal, colored lights began to shoot through it, red and blue, blue, then red. "Here," said Grassina walking over to set the scale in the basket, propping it against the side so I could see my reflection in its shiny surface. "As the bracelet's rightful owner, place your hand on the scale and determine which direction we must go."

My stomach flip-flopped when Grassina picked up the basket, and I grabbed the sides to keep my balance. I waited until my footing was secure before reaching for the scale. Black as the deepest night, it was as thick as my father's thumb and as wide across as the palm of his hand. The edge was serrated but for one smooth section and I was glad I didn't have to pick it up. With the surface so slick and the edges so sharp, I was sure I would have either cut myself or dropped it. "Now what do I do?" I asked Grassina, looking up at her.

"Just wait," she said. "Patience is a virtue and often vital when doing magic. The scale is seeking the otter for you. It will tell you the direction in a moment."

"You mean it's going to talk to us?" Eadric asked, pressing his eardrum against the center of the scale.

"No!" Grassina laughed. "Watch the color. Red means hot and you're going in the right direction. Blue stands for cold and will appear if you take any direction but the right one. Look, it's working."

The red lights were gone, leaving only blue to shoot about inside the scale. "It's cold, Aunt Grassina. This is the wrong direction. Turn around and we'll see what it does."

"Hot, cold, it sounds like a child's game," grumbled Eadric. "I thought the scale would tell us more than that."

Grassina smiled and shook her head. "I said it was a small favor! Besides, this will be sufficient. Now, Emma, how about this?"

My aunt began to turn in a circle, but the lights were

still blue. It wasn't until she had turned three-quarters of the way around that they began to flash red. "Now, Aunt Grassina! We have to go that way!"

"Very well! Then we'll be off." Gathering her skirts with one hand while holding the basket with the other, she started walking.

"Are you going to take us all the way to the otter?" asked Eadric, struggling to stay on his feet as the basket jiggled and bounced. "Because that's very kind if you are."

"I'm not trying to be kind. I'm just not about to let my niece go traipsing off into the swamp without me again. Not after what happened last time! Emma, keep your eye on the scale and tell me if I need to change direction."

"You're doing fine, Aunt Grassina. No, wait, you've lost it.... That's it, a little to the left ..."

I never have been a good judge of distance, but it soon became apparent that the otter wasn't to be found close by. Grassina and I worked as a team, turning this way and that as the lights changed from red to blue. Sometimes the scale took us to an unpassable point and we had to turn around and find another way. Quagmires, ponds, even an apparently bottomless pit made it impossible to go straight. It didn't help that Grassina turned around and backtracked each time we encountered flowers, looking worried until we'd circumvented the plants by a large margin.

Having crossed swampy terrain myself, I knew how exhausting it could be, but Grassina never complained, remaining cheerful even when the mud tried to suck her shoes off her feet, branches whipped her cheek, or she had to retrace her steps yet again. It wasn't until I announced that my head ached from staring at the flickering lights that she suggested we stop to rest. I was grateful on my own account and pleased that I'd found an excuse to make her rest as well.

With nowhere to sit but the sodden ground, Grassina gestured at a small hummock and whispered softly. The ground rumbled and a large stone rose out of the mound, rotating to present a flat surface. Another word from Grassina and a puff of wind scoured the rock free of soil and insects. Sighing with pleasure, my aunt settled herself on the rock and set the basket on her lap.

"Can I ask a question?" asked Eadric.

Grassina smiled. "Yes, Eadric, of course, although I'm not sure that I can answer it."

"That spell that you said earlier, the one about finding the bracelet ... Did you make that up as you went along or did you think of it ahead of time?"

"I made it up as I said it. That's how I do most of my spells."

"You're very good! I could never come up with something like that on the spur of the moment."

"It takes practice, that's all."

"Do all spells have to rhyme?" I asked.

"No. It depends on the witch, really. Rhyming works better for some, prose for others. Whatever she's comfortable with. I happen to prefer rhyming, but then I've always loved poems that rhyme. Haywood used to write the most beautiful poems for me...."

"But coming up with the right words ..."

"Comes with time and practice. It's best if novices use established spells, ones that are known to work."

"Hmm," I said. I had a lot to think about. My success with magic in Vannabe's cottage had made me look at the art in a different light. Sure, I had messed up every other time I'd tried it, but then I hadn't really believed that I could do it. But now that I knew that I could, and that I had the flair ... I had an idea, vague at first, but the more I thought about it, the more I thought it would work.

And that was another thing. I appreciated Grassina's help and I knew that it had made finding the otter easier and faster, but I wanted to see what I could do.

"Aunt Grassina, I want to get the bracelet back myself," I blurted out, certain that if I didn't say it now, I might lose my nerve. "When we find the otter, I want to be the one to talk to him."

"Emma," said Eadric. "Are you crazy?"

Grassina frowned. "But why? I'll be there. The otter won't hurt me, but it's too dangerous for a frog."

"I've come up with a plan. I want to try some magic of my own. You said yourself that I have the flair, a natural talent for magic. If I really do have the gift ..."

Eadric sputtered, trying to get the words out. "It's—it's out of the question! I told you that otters eat frogs!"

"But he won't see me as just a frog! I know what to do."

"Tell me about this plan of yours," said Grassina, looking as serious as I'd ever seen her.

"It's simple, really. I'll dress as the swamp fairy and tell the otter that the bracelet is mine and that he has to give it back. There isn't a real swamp fairy, is there, Aunt Grassina?"

"None that I know of, but I don't keep up with all the fairies in the area."

Eadric shook his head. "You're a frog, Emma! How do you think you can pass yourself off as a fairy?"

"That wouldn't be a problem," said Grassina. "Fairies are magical beings by their very nature and can easily take the form of an animal if they choose. I've met fairies who look like cats, so why not a frog?"

"What made you think of a swamp fairy, anyway?" Eadric asked.

"The otter isn't going to hand anything over to a frog, is he?" I said. "But I bet he would to a fairy. Everyone knows that fairies can be nasty if they're crossed."

Eadric snorted. "And what are you going to do if the otter doesn't laugh himself to death?"

"Use a little magic to convince him that I'm serious. I already have a few spells in mind."

"This may not be the best time to bring it up," said Grassina, "but you haven't had such wonderful results with some of your magic...."

"This won't be the same at all. I remember some of the spells from Mudine's books. I'll use one of those, more than one if I have to."

"That's your plan?" said Eadric. "It'll never work! It's too simple."

Grassina shook her head. "I don't agree with you, Eadric. Sometimes the simplest plans are the best. Things get too complicated and there are too many things that could go wrong. But Emma, I can't agree with this idea of yours, either. It's just too dangerous! You're too inexperienced. Why, you haven't even been practicing magic the way you should have."

"I know, and I'm sorry about that, but I'm sure I can do this."

"Maybe so," said Grassina, "but this isn't the time to try out your magic. Even if you were proficient, the otter could be too fast for you. No, I'll have to handle this."

My aunt isn't the easiest person to argue with. Once she makes up her mind, she refuses to listen to other people's opinions. I was going to try anyway until I

182

noticed a faraway look in her eyes and I knew that she was already thinking about what she was going to do.

Seventeen

y midafternoon we had reached the river, and it became obvious that we were getting close when we saw that the scale was filled with brilliant red lights exploding in a flurry of blazing sparks. Following the river, we came to an old willow growing halfway down the bank, its roots anchoring it to the crumbling mud that the river threatened to wash away. With the scale glowing a fiery, solid red, we knew that we'd found the otter's den.

Eadric and I peered over the side of the basket as Grassina took a step closer, and there, growing along the water's edge and completely surrounding the den, was a great swath of knee-high plants topped by clusters of clear blue blossoms. Grassina gasped, then turned and scrambled back upriver, away from the threat of the flowers.

"Oh, dear," she said, wiping a sheen of perspiration from her upper lip once she had gotten far enough away.

"That won't do at all."

"Are you all right?" I asked, not liking the way she had suddenly gone pale.

"Yes, yes, I am," she said, patting her face as if to make sure. "But I can't possibly go near the otter's den now. You saw that larkspur. If I were to touch it ..."

"I don't understand," said Eadric. "Why would you be afraid of some plants?"

"Aunt Grassina is allergic to flowers."

"I'm afraid it's not an allergy, Emma. It's a curse, placed on our family generations ago. It began with Hazel, the first Green Witch."

"But I was told that you and Mother were allergic."

"We didn't want to frighten you, but this curse affects all the women in our family, starting on their sixteenth birthday. We thought we had a few years before we had to tell you."

"What does this curse do?" asked Eadric.

Grassina shuddered and a look of horror crossed her face. "It changes a witch, and she becomes hideous. Her hair becomes coarse; her nose lengthens, growing hooked and lumpy, nearly meeting her chin. Her face and body are covered with warts, her voice turns into an ugly cackle, and her personality—"

"That sounds just like Grandmother! Do you mean it was the curse that made her look that way?"

Grassina nodded. "She didn't believe in the curse

185

until it was too late."

Eadric scratched his head with his toe, the jerking of his leg making the basket shake. "Isn't there any way to break the curse? Surely a family of witches ..."

"The curse is very old. According to the story I heard, Hazel was a lovely young woman and an already accomplished witch who threw a party to celebrate her sixteenth birthday, inviting all the local princes and princesses, witches, and fairies. Hazel had a green thumb and was known for growing the most beautiful flowers in the region. As the guests left at the end of the evening, she gave each one a bouquet that had been charmed to last a lifetime. However, some unexpected guests had arrived, so she ran short of bouquets. When the last fairy stood at the castle door having received nothing more than an apology, she cursed the witch Hazel and all her female descendents. Unfortunately, part of the curse involves an unpleasant disposition and Hazel became too surly to do anything about it. When she died, she took the solution to the curse with her. Fairies, however, live for a very long time, so the curse lives on in us. After our sixteenth birthday, we don't dare touch a flower for fear of falling victim to Hazel's fate."

"That's terrible!" said Eadric. "Don't worry, Emma. After you turn sixteen, I'll never bring you flowers."

"Gee, thanks," I said, certain he wouldn't have anyway.

Grassina wrung her hands in despair. "I'm sorry, Emma. I don't dare go near those flowers!"

"Can't you get rid of them with a spell?" asked Eadric.

"No. Even touching them with my magic would bring on the transformation!"

"It's all right," I said. "I wanted to do it myself anyway. But if you could help me get ready ..."

"Of course!" she said, but she still looked worried. "I feel very bad about this, you know. It's terribly dangerous. We'll just have to take every precaution." Grassina nodded, as if she'd come to a decision. "All right. What can I do to help?"

"First, we need to find a few things."

I would have preferred to use flower petals to make my skirt, but the curse made that impossible if Grassina was going to help. After finding velvety, heart-shaped leaves, we set about collecting the rest of my supplies. Aunt Grassina picked some broad leaves that I folded to make pouches, filling one with pine sap and another with bits of mica we chipped from a large rock. Pine needles and spiderwebs went into other pouches, and I found a straight twig that wasn't too long or too thick, one that felt just right in my hand.

I directed Grassina to a spot by the river where I had seen dragonflies zigzagging above the water on their own mysterious errands. We waited on the riverbank while Eadric caught a snack, bringing me an assortment of dragonfly wings on his return. I was just too excited to be hungry.

Once we were together again, we made our way to a sunny spot at the edge of a meadow with sun-warmed boulders to sit on and enough insects to keep Eadric happy. I tried to use the spiderweb thread to sew myself a leafy skirt, but frog fingers aren't made for holding needles, so Grassina had to do it. While she sewed, I made my magic wand, spreading pine sap on the end of the twig before dipping it into the pouch filled with bits of sparkling mica.

When I'd finished the wand, I sorted through the dragonfly wings Eadric had brought me, looking for the prettiest. After eliminating a few because they were either too big or too small, I chose a buttercup-yellow pair with pale green veining. Not only were they the right size, but they looked nice with my velvety emerald-green skirt.

Once I had the skirt on, I asked Grassina to glue the wings to my back with another dab of pine sap. They drooped a bit and we were trying to fix them when Eadric returned, his stomach bulging with all the insects he'd eaten.

"I'm ready!" I announced, although my wings still weren't quite right.

"Just a minute," said Grassina. Taking a chain from

around her neck, she showed me her farseeing ball, encased in golden filigree. She blew on it and the ball frosted over with her breath, turning milky and opaque. "Now tap it," she said, holding the sphere out to me.

I did as she ordered and my face appeared in the ball. "There," she said, making herself comfortable on the boulder. "It's focused on you now and will show me everything that goes on around you. I can watch from here. I'll know right away if you need me and I'll be there in an instant, curse or no curse."

"Grassina ... ," I began.

"It's the only way I'll let you go without me."

"That's fine for you," said Eadric, "but I'm going with her."

"You can't!" I exclaimed. "It won't work if anyone else is there."

Eadric held up his hand as if that could stop any protest. "I won't go the whole way. The otter will never see me. I just want to make sure you're all right."

I was touched by his concern. He could be so obnoxious at times, so sweet at others. Sometimes I just didn't know what to make of Eadric.

After saying good-bye to Grassina and promising her that I'd be careful, I started back to the otter's den with Eadric at my side. He seemed cheerful enough at first, but as we neared the river, his expression became grim.

"I've been thinking," he said. "Why don't we just go

in the otter's den while he's out and find the bracelet ourselves?"

"And risk having him come back and find us there? We'd be trapped in his den just waiting for him to eat us!"

"That's true," he said. "But if one of us kept him away ..."

"Eadric, we talked about this!"

"I know, but I don't think you should do it. You're not invincible, you know, and you're not as experienced as I am. You've never had to face the wrath of a charging dragon or a goblin gone berserk. I can't help it. I'm worried. If something happens to you, I'll end up a lonely old frog. Give me the swamp fairy stuff and I'll go instead."

I tried not to smile, but it wasn't easy. The thought of Eadric in the swamp fairy skirt was too funny for words, but the fact that he had offered to take my place meant a lot to me.

"That's an awfully nice offer, Eadric, but I'm afraid it wouldn't work. I don't think you'd make a very believable swamp fairy."

"I don't know. ..."

"This is going to work, Eadric. I know what I'm doing." *I hope,* I thought, trying to look optimistic. What if the otter didn't believe me? What if Grassina couldn't get there in time? The consequences of failure would be far worse than my usual humiliation, for if I didn't do this just right, the otter would eat me. If I succeeded, however, Eadric and I would be humans again before the end of the day. Either way, what happened next would determine my future, or even whether I was going to have one.

The shadows were growing longer when Eadric and I approached the otter's den. With both of us caught up in what I was about to do, we forgot to pay attention to our surroundings. When we heard the thud of running paws, we barely had time to hop for cover before the huge white dog came into sight. It was the same beast that had tried to eat me, the same one the old toad had chased away. Although we hid in the tall grass, it was obvious from the way he was sniffing the air that the dog had caught our scent and would soon find us.

"What are we going to do?" I whispered to Eadric. "If I go in the water now, my costume will be ruined and I'll have to start all over again!"

"Don't worry." said Eadric. "I'll handle this. Look for the otter's den under the willow's roots. I'll meet you back here as soon as I get rid of the dog. Just make sure you get that bracelet back!"

Without telling me what he was going to do, Eadric crawled out of our hiding place and hopped directly into the dog's path. "Hey, doggie!" shouted Eadric. "I'm over here!"

The dog had been snuffling the ground, but at the

sound of Eadric's voice, its head jerked up. Eadric began to hop about erratically to get the dog's attention. I watched in horror as the beast spotted Eadric and bounded after him, its tail wagging so hard that it was just a blur.

"There you are! I've been looking all over for you!" said the dog.

Eadric took off, hopping faster than I would have thought possible.

"Hey!" yelped the dog. "Wait for me!"

They were well down the path before I knew what had happened, and although I wanted to go after them to stop Eadric from sacrificing himself, I realized that not only would it be useless, but it was already too late. Eadric was a much better hopper than I was and I could never catch up with them. The only thing I could do was follow my plan and get the bracelet back. With any luck, Eadric and I would both be successful and we really would meet back in the tall grass.

Worrying about Eadric made it harder to concentrate. I'd thought I'd gotten to know him during our travels, but I would never have expected him to be so brave. Eadric, of all people! For the first time I began to believe that his boasts might not have been unfounded after all.

Watching for some sign of either Eadric or the dog, I left my hiding place and hopped to the old willow tree, sitting down beside the half-concealed entrance to the otter's den. I hadn't been waiting long when the otter appeared, a fat fish flopping between his jaws. When the otter saw me, his eyes grew wide and his mouth dropped open. The fish he had been carrying fell to the ground, thrashing and gasping for air.

"Who in the name of all that's edible are you?" asked the otter.

"I am the swamp fairy!" I announced in what I hoped was a confident and convincing voice.

"You are, huh? You look like a frog, and to me that means supper. I do believe in big meals. There's always room for more."

"Don't be impertinent," I said, holding my head high. "It's never a good idea to insult a fairy. I'm here because you have something that belongs to me."

"Really?" said the otter. "And what's that?"

"My bracelet. You took it from the pond and I want it back!"

The otter laughed, a high, twittering chirp that ordinarily would have made me smile. "Sorry, you're not getting anything from me that way. Give me a reason I should think you're the swamp fairy and not the second course of supper."

"You asked for it," I said, flinging a handful of the sparkling mica dust into the air for an impressive effect. The otter drew back and winced, using his paw to wipe the dust from his eyes. I coughed and wiped my own eyes as well, for I'd neglected to take the breeze into account and half the dust had blown in my direction.

My eyes were watering as I pointed my magic wand at the otter. Thankful that I didn't have to read just then, I recited one of the spells I had read in Vannabe's cottage:

> Be gone ye old and dingy hue,
> Erase the old, bring on the new!
> Bright and shiny, lustrous locks,
> Make it look real, not from a box.

The spell, Hair So Nu, hadn't been intended for otters, so I decided to customize it.

> Redo yon fur to shades of blue!
> And make the color ever true!

With the sound of tiny cymbals and a flash of blue light, the otter's fur turned a nice shade of turquoise.

"Aagh!" screamed the otter. "What have you done to me?"

"I thought you needed a little convincing. Now do you believe that I'm the swamp fairy?"

The otter snorted. "I don't know if you're the swamp fairy or just some overdressed frog, but either way I'm not giving that bracelet to you! What would you do with it anyway? The thing is almost as big as you are! You can forget it!"

"What if I make all of your fur fall out?" I bluffed. "What will you do in the winter?"

The otter glanced down at his thick pelt and shivered. When he looked up, he seemed resigned, although none too happy. "You drive a hard bargain. Wait here, I'll get the bracelet. The light from the darn thing was keeping me awake at night anyway."

I was so excited, I hugged myself with glee as the otter trudged down the entrance to his den. The sound of thumping and scrabbling came from the tunnel, and then he reappeared, his blunt muzzle speckled with dirt. Frowning his displeasure, he shoved the bracelet into my hands. It was bigger than my head and would fit easily around my neck, but I was afraid it would choke me if I suddenly turned back into a human. Although I knew it was supposed to take a kiss to turn me back, just holding the bracelet made me nervous. After all, it had already done something unexpected once. I stared at it, trying to decide what to do.

"Well?" said the otter. "Did you want something else?"

"No, no, that was it," I said, backing away. "You may go about your business again, otter."

"Huh," said the otter, scratching his head. "Fairy or not, you sure are a strange one!"

Clutching the bracelet, I hopped back along the riverbank to the tall grass where I had last spoken with Eadric, but he was nowhere in sight. I started to call his name until I realized how dangerous that would be. If the dog was somewhere around, the last thing we wanted to do was attract its attention. We were still frogs, after all, and still needed to be careful. I waited in the tall grass for the longest time, getting more and more worried, until I heard the slap of something wet landing on the mud behind me, nearly making me jump out of my skin.

"So you got it! I knew you would!"

I whipped my head around and my knees went weak with relief. "Eadric! You got away from the dog! How did you do it?"

Eadric smiled smugly and tapped himself on the chest. "I'm a better swimmer, that's how. No dog can keep up with me!"

I grinned and threw my arms around his neck in a big froggy hug. "I was so worried!"

"Why?" he asked, frowning. "I told you I'd meet you here. Now put on that bracelet before we lose it again!"

"Is something wrong?" said a voice, and I looked up to see Grassina striding through the grass.

I shook my head and grinned up at her. "Not a thing! In fact, everything is perfect! Look, I got the bracelet!" I held it up to show her. It was so big it took both of my hands to lift it.

Grassina smiled back at me absentmindedly, as if she were thinking about something else. "I know. I saw. You did very well."

"I'd like to get a little farther from the otter before I put it on, though, just in case he changes his mind."

"Good idea," said Grassina. "Although I don't think he will. Excuse me, I'll be back in a few minutes. There's something about that otter..." She walked away in a daze, not noticing the prickers that caught at her skirts as she passed.

I would have followed her or tried to make her come with us, but Eadric grabbed my arm and tugged. "Come on," he said. "Let's get this over with."

"Fine, but as soon as we're back to normal, we have to find my aunt. She looks so odd...."

"Stop right there!" said an authoritative voice. A glimmering light descended from the sky and settled on the ground. The light swirled and shifted into the form of a fairy, her blue hair streaked with gray, her violet-colored eyes looking tired and slightly bored. Enormous, iridescent wings of violet and mauve fanned the air behind her. When she took a step toward us, her long blue flower-petal skirt, browned and curling at the edges, rustled around her ankles. Bending down, she stretched out her hand and said, "That bracelet belongs to me now!"

I gasped. "Who are you?"

The fairy glared at me. "I am the swamp fairy! The real, one and only, honest-to-goodness swamp fairy! I was told that someone was impersonating me! What is the world coming to? A fairy goes away on vacation for a couple of decades and suddenly everybody tries to take advantage.... Shame on you! I have to fine you for that! Hand over the bracelet!"

I took a step back. "What do you want with my bracelet?"

The fairy looked me over as if I might be hiding something. "It seems to be the only thing you have of any value, so that's how you'll pay your fine."

"No, wait! I can't give you this bracelet!" I said, clutching it to my chest. "We really need it! Isn't there anything else I can give you?"

"Nope, that's it. I don't need any firstborn tadpoles, if that's what you're thinking. So give me the bracelet and be on your way."

I couldn't do it, not when we were so close! Panicking, I turned to look at Eadric and my eyes fell on the vial of dragon's breath. "I know! Eadric, turn around!" I hurriedly untied the twine holding the vial on Eadric's back.

"I thought you said there wasn't any swamp fairy," Eadric whispered.

"I didn't think there was," I whispered back.

"But how do we know she's—"

"Eadric, don't say another word! You're going to get us in even more trouble!"

"I can hear you!" trilled the swamp fairy. "Hasn't anyone ever told you that it's not polite to whisper? Now I have to raise your fine!"

"Sorry," I said. "Here, would this do instead of the bracelet?" I held the vial in the sunlight so the fairy could see the beautiful swirling colors.

"What is it?" asked the swamp fairy, looking skeptical.

"It's a vial of dragon's breath. I understand it's very valuable."

"Dragon's breath? I haven't seen any of that in ages! Here, let me have it!"

I started to pass the vial to the swamp fairy, but I was fumble-fingered and it slipped out of my hand. My heart jumped into my throat when the vial landed with a thud on her foot.

"Ow! Ow! Ow! Ow!" she said, hopping on one foot while cradling the other in her hand. "You dropped it on me! Ow! Ow! Ow!"

Eadric and I backed behind a clump of grass, trying to stay out from under the hopping fairy. "I'm sorry!" I said, feeling like an idiot. "I didn't mean to!"

"Never mind that!" said Eadric. "Is the vial all right?"

The swamp fairy gave him a nasty look. Ignoring Eadric, I hurdled over the grass and bent down to pick up the vial. When I offered it to the fairy, she snatched it from my hand and gave me a nasty look as well.

The fairy uncorked the vial and sniffed it cautiously. Her face promptly turned a bright green. Coughing, she rammed the cork back into the opening. "Hoo-wee! Does that stuff ever stink! That's dragon's breath, all right. Sure, I'll take this as your fine. I have a good friend who's a dragon. He's getting old and fat and has been short of breath for years. This would make a great birth-day present for him. But now you have another fine to pay. Two, come to think of it. One fine for whispering about me, and the other for hurting my foot! What else have you got that you can give me?"

"Why, nothing, other than the bracelet."

"Then I'd better take that as well. It is awfully pretty...." Grabbing the bracelet, the fairy turned it over and shook it, smiling when the light danced on the little symbols.

"But we need it!" Eadric wailed. "Without that bracelet, we'll be stuck as frogs forever!"

"Really?" said the fairy. "What does this bracelet have to do with you being a frog?"

I didn't want to tell her, but Eadric had already said too much. I couldn't see any harm in telling her the rest. "I was a human until I kissed Eadric, but I was wearing the bracelet...."

The fairy's eyes opened wide. "And the bracelet

200

turned you into a frog?"

I nodded. "Yes, it's a—"

"Here! Take it!" she said, thrusting the bracelet at me. "The last thing I want to do is turn into a frog! Imagine, me as a hairless, slimy—"

"Hey!" said Eadric, scowling at the fairy. Afraid of what he might say, I jabbed him in the stomach with my elbow.

"But that's all we have," I said.

The fairy took a step back. "Never mind. The dragon's breath will do just fine. If you promise never to impersonate me again, I'll forget your other offenses and we'll call it even."

"Oh, I promise!" I said.

Eadric and I hopped away from the river as if a dragon were after us. Faster than you can say "four fat frog feet" five times fast, we had jumped through a small copse of saplings and into a nearby meadow.

"Now can you put it on?" Eadric asked as soon as he'd caught his breath. "I hate to be pushy, but something else is bound to happen if you don't."

"Just a minute," I said, setting the bracelet on the ground. Since the bracelet seemed to remain the same size no matter what, I wasn't going to take any chances. I sat down, placed my wrist inside the bracelet, and patted the ground. "Eadric, have a seat over here."

Eadric hurried to sit beside me. "I'm ready," he said, puckering his lips.

"Let's hope this works!" I crossed my fingers and leaned over to kiss him.

I saw movement out of the corner of my eye and looked up to see the dirty white dog trotting into the meadow, its nose held high as it snuffled the air. A sparrow shot from the ground by the dog's feet, but the beast swung its head from side to side as if homing in on a scent, oblivious to everything else. I tried to ignore the dog as I kissed Eadric long and hard on the lips. When nothing happened right away, Eadric's face drooped in disappointment and I felt as though I was about to cry.

A breeze blew from behind us, carrying our scent directly toward the dog. With his ears pricked forward, he swung his head in our direction and trotted toward us, his tail wagging like a flag. Resigned to certain doom, I was watching the dog when my fingers and toes began to tingle. The feeling spread up my arms and down my legs. A shiver ran along my spine, chased by the golden, fuzzy feeling. Once again my head felt light and full of bubbles. Once again a tremendous wind rushed past me and I fell to the ground with a gray cloud filling my head, but not before I saw the dog collapse as well.

Eighteen

When I woke, my head felt woozy; nothing would come into focus. Gradually my vision sharpened, but everything looked different. The colors seemed duller and there were fewer of them. I shook my head, trying to get rid of the funny feeling in my ears, not liking the way the sounds were muffled. Glancing down, I saw that my clothes looked just the way they had on the day I had turned into a frog. My blue gown and kirtle were only slightly soiled, but no more than they had been when I kissed Eadric. My soft leather shoes were still damp, the mud on them fresh.

I heard a sound and turned to see Eadric struggling to sit up beside me. He was wearing a warm traveling cloak over his clothes, and his boots were splattered with muck. His tousled brown curls framed a strong jaw, laughing eyes, and a nose as prominent as my own. He was slightly pudgy and rather short. I thought that he was the most beautiful person I had ever seen.

Eadric looked at me and grinned. "We did it!" he said, laughing out loud.

"Finally!" I agreed. I had been convinced so often over the last few days that I was about to die that I felt giddy with relief now that I was a human again.

"You look beautiful, Emma."

"You do, too."

"But aren't you tired of wearing those wings?" He reached behind me and tugged something loose from the back of my dress. The dragonfly wings lay in his hand, limp and broken.

"Oh," I breathed, taking the wings from him. "I'll cherish them forever."

"Those old things!" said Eadric. "Why would you want to keep them?"

"Eadric, how can you say that? They made me look like a beautiful swamp fairy!"

When I tried to stand, my movements were stiff and awkward. I took a step and tripped over my own feet, landing in Eadric's arms. He held me with my head cradled on his shoulder so that I was looking up into his eyes.

"I was hoping I could get another kiss," he said, his eyes laughing.

"You never give up, do you? Well, I'm sorry! I'm not kissing anybody until I get this back to my aunt Grassina!" I raised my arm and jingled my bracelet next to his ear. "I don't want to—"

"—take any chances," Eadric finished for me.

"We'd better be careful or we're going to end up finishing each other's sentences like Clifford and Louise."

"Who?" Eadric asked.

"Never mind. I'll tell you all about it when we have the time."

Something snorted, sounding like the chuffing of an ancient dragon. Startled, Eadric and I looked up. A white horse with a silver mane lay on its side, trying to roll to its feet. Saddled for riding, it wore the trappings of royalty.

"Eadric! Why did you run away?" whinnied the horse.

"Brighty?" said Eadric, shading his eyes against the sun. "Is that you?"

"Who's Brighty?" I asked.

"My horse, Bright Country! I left him tied to a tree while I hunted for the meadwort and that's when I ran into Mudine. I was so worried about you, boy!"

With a lunge and a flurry of hooves, Brighty rolled to his feet and stood with his legs wobbling beneath him. "Dang, I'm sore!" he grumbled. He snorted again and looked toward Eadric, who dumped me on the ground and climbed painfully to his feet.

"Hey!" I said, struggling to sit up. "Why did you do that?"

"I've got to go. It's Brighty!"

I looked at his horse again. There was something about ... "That's where the dog was standing when we kissed!" I said. "The big white dog that was chasing you!"

"You don't suppose that Mudine cast a spell on Brighty, too?"

"I guess it's possible! Then the reason the dog was chasing us ..."

Eadric stumbled toward his horse. "Brighty! I always knew you were a good and faithful beast! You wanted to be with me, even when I was a frog!" With a happy sigh, Eadric flung his arms around the horse's neck and hugged him. Brighty leaned into his owner, making the prince stagger back.

The horse snorted, his breath ruffling Eadric's hair. "I've been looking for you everywhere! I saw that woman turn you into a frog; then she came after me. I was a dog, Eadric! You can't imagine what it was like. I had this urge to sniff everything! And some things were really disgusting and I didn't want to eat them, but I couldn't help myself. I'm so glad I found you. I knew if I did, everything would be all right. Don't ever leave me like that again!"

"Everything will be fine now, Brighty. I'm here," said Eadric, hugging his horse again.

I smiled and let out an unladylike snort of my own. "I bet your horse would kiss you if you let him."

"I wouldn't dare," said Eadric. "With all the magic that's been floating around here today, there's no telling what might happen."

"Speaking of magic, we'd better go see what happened to my aunt. That look on her face—it was almost like someone had cast a spell on her! And she was going toward those flowers ..."

Leading Brighty by the reins, Eadric followed me through the meadow to the riverbank. Everything looked so much smaller than it had when we were frogs that I felt as though we'd entered a different world. The weeds that had shaded us from the heat of the sun now brushed against our ankles. I almost missed the clump of tall grass, for now it rose no higher than my knees. It was disconcerting to see the world so radically changed, and I know it bothered Eadric as much as it did me, because I caught him rubbing his eyes and staring at what we would once have considered an enormous butterfly, but now it seemed only average.

I heard voices talking as we neared the willow. I even thought I heard Grassina's laugh. After persuading Eadric to tie his horse's reins to a convenient branch, I hiked up the hem of my gown and clambered awkwardly over the uneven ground in search of my aunt Grassina. Still following the voices, we passed the den, and there, just beyond a jumble of rocks that jutted into the river, I found her with the otter curled at her feet. She glanced up at the sound of our approach, and I was stunned. Her smile was filled with so much joy that even her eyes sparkled with it.

"He wasn't a frog at all!" she said, taking the otter's paw in her hand. "That's why I couldn't find him. I kissed all those frogs for nothing! My mother turned him into an otter! Emma, Eadric, I'd like you to meet Haywood, my betrothed!"

Haywood tore his gaze from Grassina and looked up at me. "So you're Grassina's niece! The family resemblance is extraordinary! And you must be her beau, Eadric! Grassina has been telling me about you both."

"I'm not her beau, exactly," Eadric said, turning to look at me.

"I saw Haywood in the farseeing ball," said Grassina, "and I had a feeling that it was him. I felt the way I do when someone comes to the door and I know who it is before I open it. Then when I saw him up close ... The spell changed his shape, but it couldn't change who he was inside."

"If it was that easy, why didn't you know it was us when we came to your door?" Eadric said, looking indignant. "You made Emma tell you the whole story and then you said you still weren't sure it was her!"

"Because my heart told me that it was Emma at the door, but my head said that she couldn't possibly be a frog. She wore the bracelet, so I didn't think it was possible. But I know to trust my heart now and my heart says that this is the same darling Haywood whom my mother sent away."

"I am a bit older, though, I'm afraid," the otter said, patting her hand with his other paw.

"Not so old, Haywood. No older than I."

The otter gazed into my aunt's eyes. "My darling Grassina, I wish we could go back to the way things were. That's all I've wanted for these many years. Do you think it's still possible?"

"Oh, Haywood," said Grassina, "I would like that more than anything in the world!"

"Kiss her," said Eadric, "and see what happens!" He grinned and turned to look at me. Seeing the surprised expression on my face, he added, "Well, it worked for us, didn't it?"

"Not at first! Aunt Grassina, you aren't wearing any charm reversal jewelry, are you? No bracelets or necklaces or anything like that?"

"No, Emma, I'm not...."

"Then what are you waiting for?" Eadric asked, rocking back and forth on the balls of his feet as if he couldn't possibly hold still.

"Nothing," Grassina said, and bent down till her mouth was only inches from Haywood's. Her hair fell forward to hide their faces, but they both had dreamy looks in their eyes when they finally drew apart. We waited for a while, watching Haywood for any sign of change. As time dragged on and we realized that nothing was going to happen, Haywood's face fell and Grassina let out a heartfelt sigh.

"I didn't really expect it to work," said Haywood, "but I was hoping ..."

Only a few weeks before, I probably would have thought it bizarre to see my aunt and an otter looking at each other with such adoration, but living as a frog had made me much more sympathetic.

"I know what we can do!" I said, too excited to keep quiet any longer. Everyone turned to look at me, but I plowed on, convinced that I was right. "Haywood, do you remember what my grandmother said you had to do to break the spell?"

The otter shook his head. "I'm sure she told me, but it's been so long. Something about dragon's breath and the lining of some seashell."

"Drat!" I said. "I knew we'd find a use for that vial! But that's all right, because the spell can still be undone by the witch who cast it in the first place. All you have to do is go see Grandmother."

"What makes you think she would do it?" asked Haywood. "She probably won't like me any better now than she did before."

"She'll do it, you'll see! You'll just have to explain things to her the right way. Every time we visit her, she complains that she has only one grandchild—me. But if she changed Haywood back and you two got married ..."

"Then she could have more grandchildren!" exclaimed Eadric. "Unless you're too old ..."

"Eadric! Please!" said Grassina, blushing a deep shade of pink, a color I'd never seen on my aunt.

"I think Emma's idea is wonderful!" Haywood declared. "And after Grassina and I are married, I'll return to my studies. Perhaps we can open a practice together, just as we'd planned!"

From the way Grassina and Haywood looked at each other, I knew that Eadric and I were in the way. But there was something I had to do before we left.

"Here," I said, removing the bracelet and handing it to Grassina. "Although it's a lovely bracelet, I don't think I'd ever be comfortable wearing it again."

"I don't blame you," my aunt said, taking her eyes off Haywood only long enough to drop the bracelet into the pouch attached to her gown.

"And if I were to kiss someone now ..."

"Hmm? Oh, you wouldn't turn into anything."

"Good!" I said. "Then it's finally over! I just have one other question. Why can Eadric and I still talk to animals even though we're human again?"

"Because you've been animals yourselves. Since you're a witch, Emma, you'll keep the ability, although

Eadric may lose it if he doesn't practice often. Is there anything else?" Grassina asked, flicking her eyes in my direction. I knew her well enough to take the hint.

"Not a thing! Come on, Eadric. Let's go!"

Although I would have liked to have left gracefully, Eadric and I were both so stiff that we had to help each other up the hill. When we reached the top, I saw an ancient oak whose graying bark bore a small carved heart surrounding the words *Grassina & Haywood forever*. It made me realize that Haywood had probably missed Grassina as much as she had missed him.

Now that I knew the truth about Haywood, things that I hadn't noticed before seemed obvious. Passing his den on our way to fetch Bright Country, I saw a patch of dry grass by the opening that looked remarkably like a doormat. A collection of roughly assembled twigs resembled a crude bench. Lavender, rosemary, and thyme grew in neat little rows on the side of the hill like a miniature herb garden. Haywood may have been turned into an otter, but he had gone to a lot of trouble to make his den into a vaguely human home.

After collecting Bright Country, we made our way back along the riverbank, too sore to move much faster than a slow shuffle. We hadn't gone far before Eadric and I stopped to stretch our aching muscles. "And what about us?" Eadric asked, trying to work the stiffness out of his shoulders.

"Well, now that that's settled, I can get started on all the other things I have to do."

"Such as?"

"Such as this," I said. Eadric's eyes grew wide when I slid my arms behind his neck and kissed him. It wasn't a quick kiss like the first one that had turned me into a frog, or the lip-crushing kind that was intended to turn us back, but a long, slow kiss that was soft and gentle and very sweet.

"Wow!" said Eadric, his eyes as big as fruit tarts. Somehow, his arms had found their way around me while we kissed, and it was a very pleasant feeling indeed.

"Oh, my!" I agreed, having enjoyed it as much as he had.

"And now what?" he asked, grinning boyishly.

"And now ... Now I have to have the moat cleaned out."

"And marry that jerk, Prince Jorge?"

"Of course not! I'll just tell my mother that I won't marry him. If she insists, I'll inform her that I can't wait to tell his parents all about my adventures as a frog. My mother would never live that one down. And if he's lucky, maybe Jorge'll find the perfect woman for him, one who wears the same size shoes he does."

"His feet are kind of small. It might take him a while to find her."

"I'm sure he'll manage. People like him always do."

"You know, I've been thinking. You could tell your mother that you met someone else you'd rather marry."

"Is that a marriage proposal, Prince Eadric?"

"Would you say yes if it were, Princess Emeralda?"

"Maybe, but I don't think I'll get married just yet. I have the potential to be a very good witch, and I think it's about time I began working at it. And even if I do decide to get married later on, being a witch could be very helpful."

My days as a frog had taught me many things, most of which I'd long suspected. The swamp was indeed a magical place where old lives could end and new lives could take the most unexpected turns, where friends and heroes could come in many forms, and where life could be wonderful, even for a clumsy princess.

Eadric reached out to tuck a loose curl behind my ear. "Fine. Just promise you'll never turn me into some loathsome creature if we happen to disagree."

"I promise I won't turn you into anything you don't deserve," I said. "Just don't ever try to stop me from visiting the swamp from time to time."

"Is that all it would take to keep you happy?"

"No, but it's a good start!"

*E*mma and Eadric may be human again . . . but their magical adventures are only just beginning! Can they reverse an old spell and save the kingdom of Greater Greensward from peril?

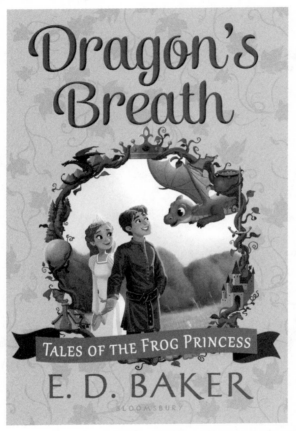

Read on for an excerpt from **Dragon's Breath**, the second book in E. D. Baker's delightful Tales of the Frog Princess series.

When I was a little girl, I dreamed about being a witch like my aunt Grassina. I imagined that the next time a page stuck out his tongue at me, I'd wiggle my fingers and turn him into a salamander. If my nurse nagged me about the dirt on my clothes, I'd say a magic word and her voice would become a sparrow's chirp. If my mother scolded me for being clumsy and sent me to my chamber, I'd wave my hand, banishing her to some far-off cave guarded by trolls. I never did these things, of course, but I comforted myself with the thought that someday everyone who had been mean to me would be sorry. Someday I would be a witch and no one would dare tell me that I wasn't as smart or pretty or graceful as a princess ought to be.

Lately, I had decided that those dreams were a waste of time. Although my grandmother and aunt were both witches, my mother hated magic and let everyone know it. According to her, no self-respecting princess would ever be interested in magic, not if she really wanted to make something of herself. She threatened to send me to a convent if she ever saw me try it. "They'll know how to keep you too busy for such nonsense," she told me more than once.

If it hadn't been for my aunt Grassina, I might have given up my dream entirely, but she said I had a talent that shouldn't be ignored. I resolved not to tell my mother I planned to study magic, and my attempts remained a secret between my aunt and me.

In a way, I owed all the excitement in my life to my mother. Because she never seemed to want me around, I'd often wandered off to the swamp or to my aunt's tower chamber. Then, when my mother had tried to get me to marry a prince I couldn't stand, I hid in the swamp, unwilling to meet with him. There I met Eadric, a prince who'd been turned into a frog. I'd ended up kissing Eadric, and that kiss had turned *me* into a frog as well.

The morning after I returned home as a human, I was eager to work on my magic, if only to gain more control over my suddenly crazy life. I had never learned how to cook, so I thought I'd use a spell to make break-fast for Grassina and my no-longer-a-frog-friend Prince Eadric. I chose a recipe from one of Grassina's books, *Wolanda's Big Book of Recipes, Potions and Cooking Spells for the Inexperienced Witch*—"time-tested, witch-approved." It was a simple spell, one that even I should have been able to handle.

After fetching some peacock eggs from the kitchen, I hurried up the tower stairs to my aunt's rooms. Since my aunt often cooked her own meals, she already had everything else I needed. According to the directions, all I had to do was assemble the ingredients and the cooking spell would do the rest.

Li'l Stinker, a bat who had become a friend in my days of being a frog, greeted me at the door. The room was quiet; my aunt was probably still sleeping.

I'd decided to use Grassina's magic pot. Made of iron and black with age, it heated itself until the food was cooked. I'd never known Grassina to burn anything when she used the pot, and I hoped the same would be true for me.

Glancing from the pot to the book and back again, I was careful to read the spell aloud exactly as it was written.

A pinch of this, a dash of that
A hint of lard, a dab of fat
A broken egg, no, make it three
One's not enough, as you can see.

Drop them in a cooking pot.
Add some spice, no, not a lot.
Chop an onion, put it in.
Stir it once, then stir again.

Heat the pot until it cooks,
Sniff, then see how good it looks.
Get the dishes, serve it all.
Don't let the portions be too small!

Cooking spells are fun to watch, but I enjoyed watching Li'l even more. She chortled when the eggs cracked themselves and plopped into the pot. I heard her gasp when the onions broke into small pieces, then spiraled into the mixture with the spices.

When I read *sniff*, the steam rising from the eggs wafted toward my nose, drifting past Li'l. "Smells good," she said, breathing deeply. "Now what do you do?"

"I'll taste them, just to be sure they're all right. Then we'll invite Grassina and Eadric to breakfast."

Although I'd used only three eggs, the magic recipe had doubled them, so there was more than enough for everyone. Wondering if it had doubled the spices as well, I nibbled a tiny morsel. It needed salt, so I glanced toward the shelves holding my aunt's supplies. A small salt cellar rested on a high shelf beside jars of dried herbs. Pleased by my success with the cooking spell, I pointed at it and said, "Salt cellar," expecting it to fly into my hands. Straightforward and simple—I didn't think anything could possibly go wrong.

Whoosh! A damp breeze whisked me from the stool where I'd been sitting, twirled me until I was dizzy and plopped me down on a lumpy sack somewhere cold and dark. Dazed, I shook my head and looked around. It could have been worse. At least I knew where I was: my parents' dungeon. And the door was most certainly locked.

I'd visited the dungeon often, but always dressed warmly and carrying a torch. It wasn't safe to walk around the dungeon in the dark. Unseen hands moved barrels, holes appeared where none had been before and doors that were centuries old suddenly disappeared. Witches had lived in the castle for generations, and here, where the early witches had set up their workshops, the magic had permeated the walls and still floated about in currents and eddies that smelled like rotting vegetables.

My mother, who wasn't a witch, had ordered the

dungeon cleaned out and now used it just for storage. But the witches' ghosts remained to haunt the old dungeon, and not all of them were friendly. My mother didn't believe in ghosts and kept the salt in the room where I now found myself, a long, narrow room that had once been used as the torture chamber. Why had I wanted salt for the eggs?

The torture chamber had no windows; not even the faintest glimmer disturbed the inky dark. I thought about using magic to go back upstairs, but I didn't know any spells that would take me from one place to another. Though I wanted to practice my magic, I didn't think I was ready to try to come up with my own spells yet, especially since it was a simple spell that had brought me to the dungeon. To get out safely, I needed some sort of light. A tethered witches' light would have to do, even though it would be vulnerable to the old magic wafting through the dungeon.

One of the first spells my aunt had taught me was for creating such a light. I'd used it many times, but only when Grassina was around. I recited the spell, shaping my hands as if I was holding a ball.

Create a glow to chase the dark.
A light to help me see.
Let neither wind nor rain nor snow
Take it away from me.

The space between my hands began to glow a rosy shade of pink as a ball of gentle light took form. I released the ball, and it drifted above my head.

I'd started toward the door when a whisper of sound behind me made me turn to look. A swirling mist glowing a faint blue poured through a hole in the wall. As the mist filled the room, a young woman appeared only a few feet away, her long tresses lifting in a nonexistent breeze. She gazed at me through shadowed eyes, her lips moving, her hands reaching in a pleading sort of gesture. An aura as cold as a winter's night surrounded her, giving me goose bumps as she drew near. Her lips moved again, and I strained to hear her words.

"I'm sorry," I said, tilting my head so that I might hear her better. "Could you repeat that?"

The ghost sighed and dropped her arms to her sides. "Then listen carefully this time," she yelled. "I *hate* repeating myself. I said, 'Help, help, save me. The executioner is coming and I've done nothing wrong.'" She spoke in a matter-of-fact sort of way, as if reciting lines that she'd repeated too often.

"Too late!" said a voice by the far wall. "I'm already here!" A broad-chested ghost dressed all in black materialized before us. His eyes glowed crimson through holes in the hood covering his head. Silently, the executioner wielded an axe, its blade dark with blood. The young lady shrieked and started to run. I closed my eyes, and when

I opened them, her head lay on the floor, gazing up in silent reproach.

"That was pretty good," I said, "although it works better when you delay your entrance, Cranston. It's more effective when Margreth convinces me of her innocence first."

"Sorry," said the executioner. "We're both a bit off today. We've had so many visitors lately, stomping around in heavy boots and thrusting torches in dark corners."

"Why were they here?" I asked.

Cranston shrugged. "Looking for something, I suppose. We're much better with the torture scene. Would you like to see that one? It's more realistic."

"No, thanks," I said, never having cared for the gruesome historic reenactments that some of the ghosts enjoyed. "I have too much to do this morning."

The ghosts disappeared, leaving me alone once again. I was stepping into the next room when my witches' light dimmed so much that I could hardly see. Something scrabbled against the stone floor like scores of metal-hard claws. I took another step, hoping to take the light out of the drifting pool of magic that had muted its glow.

A large shape loomed out of the dark, its glowing red eyes unblinking. If I hadn't encountered the creature before, I would have been terrified, but Grassina had shown me how to deal with it on one of our early visits. It was a shadow monster left behind by one of my ancestors and could be deadly to anyone who didn't know its weakness. I took one more step into the room, and the creature charged. It was almost upon me when I danced aside, rapping it between the eyes with my clenched fist. As the eyes were its only vulnerable spot, the shadow beast whined and fled into the old torture chamber.

I took another tentative step, not caring to fall into a bottomless pit or tread on a magic serpent created by an old spell. My witches' light grew brighter, lighting the darkened niches. I was halfway across the floor when a pale glow played around the edge of a door, outlining it in an eerie blue light. The light pulsed and wavered, seeming to seep through the door itself. It grew stronger the closer it came, finally taking on the shape of a man, taller than most, with shoulder-length white hair and finely chiseled features. Although the image remained translucent, I recognized him right away.

"Grandfather, you're back! I thought you were still away on ghostly business." I smiled up at the holes where his eyes should have been.

Clammy fingers touched my hand; the scent of old leather grew strong. "My darling Emma!" he answered, a chilly puff of air caressing my cheek. "I'm sorry I was away for so long. The meeting of the Council of Ghosts seems to last longer every year. I hear that you were away as well. Grassina told me something about a frog and a prince. You remind me of your grandmother. She was always doing the unexpected, too. Still is, from what I hear. You even look like her in a way."

"What?" I was horrified at the thought of resembling my grandmother in even the smallest detail. Although I had my father's large nose, I'd been told that with my taller-than-average height, auburn hair and green eyes I looked like my aunt Grassina. This was the first time anyone had ever compared me to my grandmother. Her long hooked nose, pointed chin, beady eyes, warts and straggly white hair were enough to frighten me, so I couldn't imagine that *anyone* would want to look like her. At least no one had ever accused me of acting like my grandmother.

"Olivene wasn't always like she is now. She was quite lovely when I married her, and was the sweetest and gentlest woman. It wasn't until your mother and your aunt Grassina were nearly grown that your grandmother changed."

"You're talking about the family curse, aren't you?"

"So you've heard about how the first Green Witch, Hazel, insulted a fairy?"

I had. It was Hazel's sixteenth birthday, and she didn't have enough everlasting bouquets to give one to the fairy. The fairy got angry and cursed Hazel: if she ever touched a flower, she'd end up nasty, like my grandmother was now. Aunt Grassina told me that the curse was still strong and that any female in our family who touched a flower after she turned sixteen would become a nasty hag.

"Oh, yes," I said.

"And you believe it?"

"Yes, of course. Why wouldn't I?" I asked.

"Because your grandmother didn't, at least not until it happened. Her mother had avoided flowers her entire life, but Olivene thought her mother was crazy, so she didn't believe her stories about the curse. After the curse changed her, your grandmother didn't care enough to do anything about it except send me to the dungeons."

"Is that how you ended up down here?"

A ghostly sigh brushed my ear. "Before the change, Olivene complained that I never took her to tournaments or balls at neighboring kingdoms anymore. I didn't know she wanted to go! I thought she was happy raising our girls and running the castle. She was always so busy with her magic. When your grandmother said that if I loved her I'd be more attentive and bring her little gifts, I tried to please her."

"You mean you're the one who gave her the flowers that turned her into—"

"Yes, I was the one. I had never heard of the curse, but ignorance is no excuse. After I gave her the flowers and she changed, she used her magic to send me to the dungeon for a few days. I could have left anytime after that, but I liked the peace and quiet."

I could understand why he'd want to stay in the dungeon. I'd heard from my mother and my aunt how they had fought when they were young, and if my grandmother had been as nasty as she was now, the dungeon would have been the nicest place in the castle.

"I haven't seen your grandmother for years, but the funny thing is, I miss her. I saw your mother the other day, though. She stopped by to see if you were here. Chartreuse doesn't come down very often, I'm sorry to say. Why was she looking for you in the dungeon?"

"Maybe because she couldn't find me anywhere else. I kissed a frog named Eadric in the swamp. Then I became a frog, too. Until yesterday, that is. That's when I kissed him again with my charm reversal bracelet on and we both turned back into humans. Eadric is a prince and he wants to marry me, but I told him we had to wait and see."

"Do you love him? Your mother says that love isn't essential in a marriage, but it really is, you know. When we were young, I loved your grandmother so much."

"I guess I love him in a way," I said. I just didn't know if I loved him enough, not after seeing how much Grassina loved her betrothed, Haywood. He'd been missing for years; my grandmother had turned him into an otter. "But I'm not ready for marriage yet. I want to study magic first. Last night Aunt Grassina told me that if I work at it hard enough, I might be the Green Witch someday!"

"Just like her mother was before her."

"Grandmother was the Green Witch?"

"Before the curse took hold she was the nicest as well as the most powerful witch around. Those are both requirements for being the Green Witch." Grandfather floated beside me when I started toward the door. "Now, how did you get down here?" he asked.

"We're going to the Old Witches' Retirement Community this morning to see Grandmother and ask her to turn Haywood back into a human. She wants more grandchildren and my parents aren't about to have any more, so I think she'll do it. But I wanted to make a special breakfast first."

"Are you sure it's wise to ask your grandmother for help? She's a stubborn woman. You're going to have a difficult time changing her mind about Haywood."

"Even she has to see how much Grassina and Haywood love each other."

We were passing through a long corridor, and I could see the stairway leading out of the dungeon at the far end.

"OooOooOooO!" wailed a voice. "I smell a maiden with hair of flame—"

"Go on with you! You can't smell the color of her

hair!" said an older and less refined voice.

"I was being poetic!" said the first voice. "You should have let me finish!"

"Oh, go ahead, then. What else were you going to say?"

"I forget now! And it's a real shame because it was going to be beautiful!" The voice grew fainter.

At the approach of the ghosts, the temperature of the room had dropped even further. "I don't think I've met those ghosts before," I began. "They seem ... ah ... ah ... ah-choo!" I knew right away that the sneeze wasn't an ordinary one. The tickling that had started in my nose filled my head, then rushed down my neck and into my entire body. I felt myself flash hot, then cold. My skin was suddenly sensitive to the air currents wafting through the dungeon, and I could clearly hear the sound of rats scurrying behind closed doors.

"Good gracious, child," said my grandfather. "What happened to you?"

"I don't know," I said, reaching for my tickling nose, but to my surprise, my nose wasn't there. "I think I ..." I patted my face, then ran my hands over the top of my head, feeling the smooth, moist, hairless skin. "I can't believe this! I've turned back into a frog! What's wrong with me, Grandfather? Can't I do anything right? I ... I ... ah-choo!" I sneezed explosively, and suddenly I was back to my normal self.

"Are you all right, Emma?"

I patted my hair into place, glad that I had hair again. "Fine, I guess. But why did I change when I sneezed?"

"I can't help you there. I don't understand magic very well."

We had reached the end of the corridor and started to climb the stairs when I felt the tickling again. Not wanting to turn into a frog, I pinched my nose. When the urge to sneeze faded, I took my hand from my face and said, "I'd better go before … ah-choo!" I'd let go only briefly, but it had been enough. I was a frog once more.

"Perhaps if you sneeze again," said Grandfather, "you might turn yourself back."

It wasn't hard to do. I took a deep breath and felt the tickling sensation in my nose. The sneeze was coming, and it was going to be a big one! "*Ah-choo!*" I shot back up to my normal size and shape, but the tickling wasn't over. "*Ah-choo!*" My stomach lurched as I turned back into a frog. Too many changes too fast were more than it could take. "*Ah-choo!*" The instant I turned into a human again, I clapped my hand to my face and squeezed my nose so hard it hurt.

"Here!" said my grandfather, reaching through the door to unlock it. "Go before you change again! I love you no matter what shape you're in, but I'd much rather have a human granddaughter than one who's a frog!"

E. D. BAKER is the author of the Tales of the Frog Princess series, the Wide-Awake Princess series, the Fairy-Tale Matchmaker series, the Magic Animal Rescue series, the More Than a Princess series, and many other delightful books for young readers, including *A Question of Magic*, *Fairy Wings*, and *Fairy Lies*. Her first book, *The Frog Princess*, was the inspiration for Disney's hit movie *The Princess and the Frog*. She lives with her family and their many animals in rural Maryland.

Visit E. D. Baker online at www.talesofedbaker.com.

Be sure to join the mailing list for book announcements and special giveaways!

Enter the magical world of
E. D. Baker!

www.talesofedbaker.com

www.bloomsbury.com
Twitter: BloomsburyKids
Facebook: KidsBloomsbury

A brand-new series from
E. D. BAKER
about a princess who's more than
what she seems—and the kingdom
whose fate rests in her hands.